"You look about as helpless as a wildcat."

He was angry. Marya could tell. But she was also beginning to discover that Craig was a man who could contain his anger. Restlessly, he moved away from her. "You can't deny it happened."

"I can make sure it doesn't happen again."

"So you're a coward?" he said.

"A coward for saying no to a man as used to having his own way as you?" she mocked. "An innovator, surely."

Unwilling amusement softened his face. "You're different, Marya, I'll say that for you. And I think a temporary retreat is in order. I need to consider my strategy. I concede this first round to you." With a casual salute, he added "See you later," and left the cabin.

SANDRA FIELD, once a biology technician, now writes full-time under the pen names of Jocelyn Haley and Jan MacLean. She lives with her son in Canada's Maritimes, which she often uses as a setting for her books. She loves the independent life-style she has as a writer. She's her own boss, sets her own hours and increasingly there are travel opportunities.

Books by Sandra Field

SANDRA FIELD

the land of maybe

Harlequin Books

TORONTO • NEW YORK • LONDON
AMSTERDAM • PARIS • SYDNEY • HAMBURG
STOCKHOLM • ATHENS • TOKYO • MILAN

Harlequin Presents first edition December 1991
ISBN 0-373-11416-8

Original hardcover edition published in 1990
by Mills & Boon Limited

THE LAND OF MAYBE

CHAPTER ONE

SHE was exactly the type of woman he most disliked.

For a moment Craig Huntingdon stood to one side of the wide carpeted passageway to assess the woman. She was the first passenger seated in the waiting area for the night flight to London, which he also would be taking; she did not look as though she was finding the wait pleasurable at all. Her slim and admittedly very beautiful legs were crossed, with one foot bobbing up and down, while her hands, ringless with long polished fingernails, were clenched in the lap of her stylish pastel suit. She was frowning.

Not that that detracted much from her looks, Craig acknowledged with a spurt of hostility that surprised him by its force. For not only her legs were beautiful. Her hair, which was a rich shade of chestnut, was pulled back from her face into a severe knot on the back of her head, a style that only a woman with her elegant bone-structure could have got away with. The high cheekbones, the sweep of forehead and the voluptuous curve of mouth could have belonged on the cover of the glossiest of the glossy magazines, as could the hands-off expression.

Sleek, sophisticated and brittle. Not the kind of female he admired. So why was he standing here gaping at her as if he had never seen a beautiful woman before?

He threaded his way through the rows of plastic chairs until he was standing in front of her, and said, 'Excuse me . . . would you mind keeping an eye on my bag while I go to the bookstore?'

*　　*　　*

5

Marya had been so deeply sunk in her thoughts that she had not noticed anyone approach. She looked up, startled, for it was as if the man standing in front of her had appeared out of nowhere, and momentarily a turmoil of confusion and pain was visible in her long-lashed eyes. 'I beg your pardon?' she faltered.

'I asked if you'd mind watching my bag while I go to the bookstore.'

His eyes were grey, not a changeable grey like hers, but the grey of slate; under a surface politeness they were disconcertingly sharp, seeming to see right through her, and not overly friendly.

He had no need to look at her like that, thought Marya: he was the one asking the favour. Suddenly filled with resentment at this intrusion into her privacy, she answered with minimal politeness, 'You can leave it here, yes.'

As though flint had struck stone, emotion flared in his eyes, an emotion Marya could not possibly have defined. 'Thank you,' he said.

Conventional words. Yet the courtesy of his reply had been exaggerated just enough to grate on her nerves.

As he bent to deposit his canvas bag at her feet she was given a close-up view of thick tawny hair, streaked by the sun, shining with cleanliness, and of impressively broad shoulders in a heavy knit sweater patterned in shades of grey and blue. Then he straightened. Briefly his eyes met hers, the instant antagonism like a clash of steel, before he strode between the ranks of chairs to join the throng of passengers going from gate to gate along the wide carpeted passageway.

A shiver ran up Marya's spine; against her will she watched his loose-limbed progress until he was lost to sight. Even more reluctantly she looked down at his bag, an unpretentious canvas bag that looked well travelled.

The address label was upside-down, so she could not see his name.

She did not need to know his name. He was nothing to her. Nothing. Or at the very most he was a warning that she should avoid even the most casual of contacts until she was home and her mission accomplished.

With some effort she forced him out of her mind, a move that then allowed all the panic, misery, hope and longing that had been with her for the past two days to rise up again and overwhelm her. A frown scoured her forehead and the toe of her prized Italian pump began to tap rhythmically against the canvas bag. Her sister's letter had caused these emotions. And what a happy, artless letter it had been!

Kathrin Hansen was nineteen, only three years younger than Marya, but, her elder sister had often thought, a decade younger in terms of experience. Kathrin was still sunny-natured and trusting, greeting life with a laugh; she was also extremely pretty. Little wonder that this Robb whom she talked about was enamoured of her. 'I'm engaged!! Isn't it wonderful???' she had written; her letters were always generously spattered with punctuation. 'His name is Robb, and he's a handsome Canadian with gorgeous black hair who thinks all my jokes are funny—so he must be in love, mustn't he? He's *very* rich as well, but you're not to worry about all these coincidences, *he's not like Tony at all*. We haven't made any plans for the wedding yet, it's been too exciting just getting engaged, and besides, Pa needs time to come around. But you'll come home to dance at my wedding, won't you, Marya?? *Do* say you will. I couldn't bear it if you didn't... all my love, and write soon!!!'

The letter ended with the illegible scrawl that Kathrin had long ago decided was a romantic way to sign her name. This time she had circled it with a design of tiny hearts intertwined with flowers.

Marya sighed. Why did history have to repeat itself with such horrible efficiency? Handsome, Canadian, black-haired and rich: a perfect description of Tony Mortimer, with whom she herself had fallen in love just as ecstatically three years ago. Tony had always laughed at her jokes. And Tony also had held out the promise of marriage.

When she closed her eyes, an image of Tony's white teeth and sparkling blue eyes mocked her behind her lids. She had been young and naïve, like Kathrin, and so she had believed Tony's protestations of undying love and fidelity, of a passion that would not let him sleep and of a bond that would last forever.

Forever had meant approximately nine weeks, she now thought cynically. Until he had got her into his bed, slaked his passion and grown bored with fidelity. And then he had dumped her. The same fate must not happen to Kathrin. She, Marya, had survived. But Kathrin might not. For one of the worst things Tony had done to Marya was to entice her to Canada, out of reach of her father's heavy-browed disapproval and her aunt's pleas for reason and a respectable wedding; and it was in Canada, a land in which she still felt a stranger, that he had dumped her. What if this Robb did the same to Kathrin?

Marya shivered. It was too awful to contemplate, and it was to prevent just that that she was flying from Toronto, where she had lived for the last three years, home to the Faroe Islands and to her family. Robb might be able to deceive sweet-natured Kathrin. But Kathrin's elder sister would be different.

Scowling to herself as she thought of what she would like to say to the rich, black-haired charmer who had bewitched her beloved sister, she heard a male voice remark sardonically, 'I promise I'll never ask another favour of you.'

Marya jumped, coming back to the present with an unpleasant jerk. The man with the tawny hair was standing in front of her. She said frostily, her accent very much in evidence, 'I wasn't frowning at you.'

He did not look convinced. 'Thanks for looking after my bag,' he added, hefting it in one hand.

It must have been quite apparent to both of them that her attention had been anywhere but on his bag. Annoyed with herself, furious with him—a fury out of all proportion to the cause—she gave him a curt nod and ostentatiously looked away.

The seats around her had filled up. From the corner of her eye she watched the man find a chair across from her and sit down, settling the bag at his feet. Gradually her anger subsided; she must be more overwrought than she cared to admit. As a distraction, she studied him surreptitiously.

He was wearing worn leather hiking boots and grey cords that were far from new, and she found herself wondering where he was going—hiking in Wales perhaps, or mountain climbing in Nepal? To be fair, she was sure he would be competent at whatever he was planning, for his slow, easy movements spoke of a self-confidence forged by experience. And he would probably do it alone; no high-powered executive jaunts for him.

Then she saw that he was smiling at her, a crooked smile that did not quite reach his eyes; he had been quite aware of her scrutiny. She looked away quickly, feeling as gauche and unsure as she had the first day she had gone to work at La Roulade, one of Toronto's most exclusive restaurants, over a year ago. There had been lots of high-powered executives at the restaurant. They went on pre-arranged adventures to exotic locations where they were herded very tactfully into jungles or deserts and then safely returned to the milieu of pin-stripe, double Manhattans, and Jaguars that were motorised rather than four-legged.

This man would not be like that.

More passengers filtered in and sat down as the attendants took over the desk and the computers. A little boy waving a toy plane ran up and down the aisles, and a pink-clad baby wailed in its mother's lap; the hands of the clock crept around the dial with excruciating slowness. Marya took out her boarding pass, clutching it in a damp palm, wishing with all her heart that the flight would leave early. Her decision to go home had been made in a flash, as soon as she had read Kathrin's letter, and the intervening two days had been so busy that she had had almost no time to think. But now, as she sat in enforced stillness and waited, her mind was tormented with all the old memories of her father's bitter anger, her aunt's anguish, and Kathrin's tears; thirty-eight months had passed since she had seen any of these people whom she so dearly loved. Nor had she seen the land she called home, the misty volcanic islands in the North Sea, the place they called the land of maybe . . .

'All passengers carrying first-class tickets, and those passengers requiring assistance, may now board Flight 376 departing for London in approximately twenty minutes. This is a preboarding announcement only.'

The man in the grey sweater stood up, stretching with lazy grace. Swinging his bag over one shoulder, he headed for the doorway that led to the plane, somehow getting there before anyone else. He was followed by the mother with the wailing baby.

Marya watched him go, all her earlier irritation instantly revived. The men who frequented the restaurant travelled first class; now the stranger had joined them.

She should not have been surprised, for, although his clothes were not those of a first-class passenger, something in his bearing definitely was. Nepal, she thought. Not Wales. Wales would be too ordinary, too accessible. He would be a man who craved challenge.

Cross with herself for spending so much time on the character analysis of a complete stranger, she waited in an agony of impatience, and ten minutes later was boarding the plane, where she showed her pass and inched her way through the first-class section. A pair of grey cords was stretched out comfortably in the bulkhead seat, the tawny head hidden behind the open pages of the *Financial Post*.

Another strike against him. Far too many of the men to whom she had been exposed in the last few months had perused the financial papers.

The line-up had stopped moving; the man lowered his paper in time to get the full benefit of her disapproving stare. 'Now what have I done?' he asked with a quizzical lift of his brow.

A young man whose earphones were emitting hard rock was ahead of Marya, and an elderly, hopefully deaf gentleman behind. She said crisply, 'The world of stock-markets and takeovers and conglomerates is, in my view, totally artificial and quite frequently immoral.'

'Real men don't eat quiche or read the *Financial Post*?'

The earphones moved two steps ahead, the young man twitching his fingers to the beat. 'Oh, I have no problem with quiche,' said Marya with a dulcet smile, and passed the curtain into the economy section.

The brief encounter had raised her adrenalin; at least this time she had not been left speechless. And how many times at La Roulade had she longed to express such sentiments? Rather unfair of her to vent a year's frustration on the man with the tawny hair. But he, she was quite sure, could handle it.

Anyway, after today she would never see him again.

Her seat, she discovered, was at the back of the plane. It was narrower, with much less leg-room than a first-class seat, and rather too close to the baby; she settled herself in for a long night.

And a long night it was, with meals at peculiar intervals, a Superman movie that in her rare intervals of sleep gave her nightmares of Tony, and a great deal of vocal exercise from the baby. Because her seat was at the back, she was one of the last ones off the plane. Heathrow Airport was a babel of different tongues in queues that crept forward step by step; in none of them did she see the tall stranger.

Then she caught a glimpse of the clock and began pushing her way through the crowds, searching for the right gate. She arrived there with ten minutes to spare, hurried down the tunnel and was greeted inside the door of the plane by a small cluster of irate businessmen speaking Norwegian and waving their boarding passes. Eventually a steward appeared and led the men away, making soothing noises. As Marya moved forward towards the first-class cabin a rather harassed stewardess appeared, who said as she checked Marya's pass, 'This flight has been overbooked, ma'am.'

Briefly Marya closed her eyes. 'You mean I can't get on?' she wavered, and in horror wondered if she was going to burst into tears.

'No, no—we'll find you a seat.' The stewardess consulted a chart and said, 'I'll be putting you in first class, though.'

Marya's shoulders sagged; she would have sat on the floor. She had thought in Toronto that once she started on her journey her emotions would calm down, and was discovering that the nearer she got to her destination, the more out of control they were. She said faintly, 'That's fine.'

The stewardess turned around. 'Right beside this gentleman, ma'am.'

Marya also turned and met the slate-grey eyes of the man with the tawny hair. She said foolishly, 'It's you.'

'Indeed,' he said agreeably. Picking up the *Financial Post* from the window seat beside him, he added, 'I do apologise—if I'd known you were to join me, I'd have disposed of this in the nearest garbage can.'

Marya flushed, sat down, and buckled her seatbelt. The door of the plane closed with a dull thud and the stewardess offered her a drink. 'Orange juice, please,' Marya said.

'And I thought you'd order champagne,' her companion murmured.

She looked him in the eye, disliking the mockery she saw there, disliking still more the proximity of his sleeve to hers. 'I hate champagne.'

With a tiny jolt the plane began taxiing backwards. 'You almost didn't make it,' he observed. 'My name's Craig Huntingdon, by the way. Do you live in Oslo, Miss...?'

He looked altogether too sure of himself; women, she decided with another flare-up of animosity, must fall over backwards for Craig Huntingdon, for he was extremely good-looking with his magnetic grey eyes, his thick, untidy hair and that devastating cleft in his chin. She said calmly, 'No,' and let the single word hang in the air between them.

His lips thinned. 'I was merely trying to be polite.'

For the past fourteen months as hostess of La Roulade, Marya had said and done all the correct things because her livelihood had depended on it. At the equally exclusive sports club where she had worked three mornings and two evenings a week, she had been a model of tact and discretion. But she no longer worked at La Roulade or at the club. If she did not feel like being polite—and there was no question that something about Craig Huntingdon brought out the worst in her—she did not have to be.

Then the stewardess anchored a tray in the armrests of her chair and brought her a tall glass of juice decorated with a slice of orange and a mint leaf. Marya smiled, said, 'Thank you,' and raised the glass to her lips.

The muscles in her throat moved as she swallowed and her profile was etched against the light. She sensed rather than saw her neighbour glance away, and thought with a quiver of amusement that he was probably not used to being given the brush-off; more often it would be the other way round. Perhaps she should tell him a change would do him good. Build his character.

She put her glass down on the tray and stared out of the window. As they began to move towards the runway, sun slanted through the plexiglass; quite unaware how this kindled streaks of flame in her smooth chestnut hair, she heard the rattle of the newspaper as Craig Huntingdon opened it and buried his nose in it.

The plane took off, and England fell away below as they headed north. Marya watched the shadows move among the clouds, knowing with a mingling of excitement and fear that she would arrive home this very day, that by evening the familiar blue and white bus would be letting her off only a few hundred yards from her father's house. In her mind she could picture every step of the narrow road that led between the houses to the small square one with the turf roof where Magnus Hansen lived. What she did not know—could not even guess—was how her father would greet her. Three years ago he had renounced her, furious with her headstrong, wilful love for a foreigner and her insistence on following that foreigner far across the sea. He had never written to her. It would be entirely in character that he had never forgiven her.

'Excuse me, ma'am.'

Marya's lashes flickered. She had no idea how long the stewardess had been standing there trying to get her attention, nor how much of her feelings had been showing on her face. 'Yes?'

The stewardess was consulting her list. 'You're Marya Hansen, travelling to Bergen?' Marya nodded. 'If you wouldn't mind staying in this seat all the way to Bergen, ma'am.' Still frowning at her list, she moved on.

'So, Miss Marya Hansen,' the man beside her said with a certain satisfaction, 'do you live in Bergen?'

He had pronounced her name correctly, stressing the first syllable in the Faroese way; she approved of this, for she objected to being called Maria. Besides, she knew she did not want to go back to thoughts of her father, who might this very day slam the door in her face. If sparring with Craig Huntingdon could take her mind off Magnus Hansen, then she would spar to the best of her ability.

'No, I don't live in Bergen,' she said demurely. 'Do you?'

'I'm from Vancouver.' He smiled at her deliberately. 'Even though the few words you've said to me have not exactly been complimentary, I still find your accent charming. You're not a native Torontonian.'

When he smiled, a fan of laughter lines spread from the outer corner of each eye in a way that was very attractive. Deciding caustically that he was no doubt aware of this, Marya fluttered her lashes, shook her head and said, 'Do you climb mountains, Mr Huntingdon?'

'Craig, please. I've been known to, yes. Why do you ask?'

'Are you going to Nepal?' she persisted.

His face hardened. 'I wish I were. But not this time. Tell me, Miss Hansen...is it Miss? Or will your husband be meeting you in Bergen?'

No one would be meeting her, not even at the bus-stop in Tjørnuvik, for no one knew that she was coming; surprise was one of the tactics by which she hoped to impress Kathrin and discompose the black-haired Robb. She smoothed her skirt and said lightly, 'I have never had the benefit of a husband, in Bergen or anywhere else.'

He looked disbelieving. 'A woman as beautiful as you, unmarried?'

Trying to suppress a quiver of pleasure that he found her beautiful, Marya announced, 'Not all of us see marriage as our sole goal in——'

She broke off, for the stewardess had reappeared, sliding a tray in front of each of them. Marya's bore a starched linen napkin, polished silverware, a glazed grapefruit centred with a red cherry, and in a small silver vase a miniature white rose. She stared at the rose in superstitious horror and forgot to say thank you.

Tony had filled the hotel room in Toronto on her first night in Canada with roses just like this one, bouquets of them on every available surface, drifts of them in every corner; it was the kind of flamboyant gesture that he loved, for all it cost him was money, and he had never suffered for lack of that. Later, of course, in the big bed, amid the cloying scent of too many flowers, he had taken her virginity; and it was in the taking that she had begun to discover the real man...

'What's the matter?'

The sharpness in Craig's tone brought Marya's head up with a jerk. She bit her lip and said in a thin voice, 'Nothing. I-I'm just not very hungry.'

His eyes bored into hers. But when he spoke his voice was unexpectedly gentle. 'Marya, has someone in your family died? Is that why you're on this plane? If so, I'm sorry if I've in any way added to your distress.'

Rudeness, innuendo or anger she could deal with, for she had had considerable practice; his gentleness disarmed her. She looked away. 'No—nobody's died,' she whispered. Only me, she thought. For something in herself had died three years ago, a quality of light-heartedness and trust that she had previously taken for granted and never would again...and Tony had been the killer. She was travelling today to share this insight with her sister, before it was too late. But she certainly could not share it with anyone else. She said more strongly, pressing the button for the stewardess, 'I'm really not the slightest bit hungry—that's all.'

'You could tell me to mind my own business. I'd prefer that to being fobbed off with a fake excuse,' Craig said evenly.

Her nostrils flared. 'Very well, then. Please mind your own business.'

The stewardess came round the corner just in time to hear this. Marya blushed and said over-loudly, 'Would you take the tray, please, I don't feel like eating. And would you mind bringing me a blanket and a pillow?'

'Certainly, madam.'

The tray was removed and she was given a soft blue blanket and a small white pillow. After reclining her seat, Marya adjusted the pillow behind her head and pulled the blanket up to her chin. Then she firmly closed her eyes.

Under the steady drone of the engines she could hear the clink of the spoon against the dish as Craig began eating his grapefruit. If his concern had been genuine—and surely it had been?—then she had been very rude to him. Once again. But what did it matter? After Bergen, they would go their separate ways, and she was long past the stage of wanting to pour out her story to every passing stranger.

She had slept very little the night before, and the seat was remarkably comfortable. First-class travel, she could see, had its advantages. Her breathing slowed and deepened.

The man next to her finished the grapefruit and demolished the *oeufs* mornay and melon *compote*. Then, reflectively sipping his coffee, he looked over at the woman next to him. The blanket had slipped to her waist and her off-white jacket had gaped open, revealing a camisole top in a shade of deep mauve that exactly matched her eyeshadow. Because her arms were crossed, the silky fabric clung to the swell of her breast; she looked infinitely desirable. Yet even in sleep her fingers were clenched.

On sudden impulse he drew the blanket up to her shoulders again, so carefully that she did not even stir. Then he pulled out his bag from under his seat, took out the book he had bought in Toronto and forced his attention to the page.

She was still asleep when the plane started the descent to Oslo's Fornebu Airport, sinking through the clouds until the dark green forests of Norway emerged below the wings. Craig hesitated, then very lightly touched her shoulder. 'We're in Oslo,' he said.

Marya's eyes flew open, wide and startled. In her dreams the plane had been flying through thick clouds of white roses whose petals had coated the windows, shutting out the sunlight. 'It's not dark,' she said stupidly, and felt her body give a reminiscent shudder.

'You'd better adjust the back of your seat,' Craig said tautly, leaning down to tuck his bag further under his chair. 'We only have a short stopover in Oslo, and then Bergen's no distance.'

It was kind—or at the very least, tactful—of him to ignore her obvious confusion. Marya made a valiant effort to pull herself together, pressing the button that elevated the back of her seat. She had to have her wits about her when she met Kathrin and Robb, or her whole trip would have been for nothing; yet the nearer she got, the more painfully the memories were attacking her.

Her companion, she was glad to notice, was reading a book. She turned away from him to stare out of the window as the red-tiled roofs and low hills of Oslo came into sight. The stopover was mercifully brief, and because the aircraft flew at a low altitude from Oslo to Bergen she had a reason to gaze out of the window at the lakes and mountains and fjords. The next descent, she thought as they circled above the skerries in the harbour, would be on Vágar, and then the two-hour bus trip would be all that separated her from home. Her nerves tightened; unconsciously she was kneading her hands in her lap.

'Will someone be meeting you here?'

She looked at Craig as if she had no idea who he was. 'This isn't my final destination,' she said stiffly.

'And you're not going to tell me what that is.'

She managed a faint smile. 'None of your business,' she murmured.

His jaw tightened. He said, and she could see he hated himself for asking, 'Won't you at least give me your Toronto address?'

Marya's nerves quivered in a way that had nothing to do with Kathrin and Robb. Furious with herself for succumbing to Craig Huntingdon's charm even to this limited extent, she said coldly, 'I have no idea when I'll be returning.' She had quit both her jobs because neither of her bosses had been prepared to give her two weeks' holiday on two days' notice; quitting had given her a great deal more satisfaction than being fired.

'Then let me give you my Vancouver address. I don't expect to be away that long.'

'I may not be back in Canada at all,' Marya said. It was the first time she had verbalised this; with a lift of her spirits she knew she would not care if she ever saw Toronto again.

'You don't have to look so damned happy about it,' Craig grated.

He sounded very angry, and again she felt that treacherous flicker of response. Tilting her chin she said warmly, 'I don't know why it should matter to you!'

'Neither do I,' he retorted, glaring at her as if he could not wait to be rid of her. 'I can be reached through Northwest Forestry Company in Vancouver—have you got that? They always know where I am. Northwest Forestry.'

'Thank you,' Marya snapped, and made no attempt to write the name down.

With two small bumps the plane landed, and the scream of the flaps made further conversation impossible. Marya scowled out of the window; and knew that the reason for her scowl was because the name of the forestry company was imprinted on her brain. But Craig looked like a man who would work outdoors, she thought with a reluctant stirring of interest; she could picture him striding along a woodland trail beneath the boughs of pine and fir, covering mile after mile with his long-limbed gait, at home in an environment very different from the noisy streets of Toronto and the subdued elegance of La Roulade. Perhaps that was the source of his confidence: the wilderness, like the sea, called for the kind of strength and endurance she could admire.

For a moment she allowed herself to wonder what might have happened had Craig Huntingdon met her under other circumstances, through friends or at a party. Would he have been as interested in her as he now seemed to be? Or did his interest stem from the boredom of flying and the pressure of a necessarily brief acquaintance?

And what of herself? Had she been less intensely preoccupied with what lay ahead, would she have told him her destination and given him her aunt's address? Because he seemed different from the moneyed men with whom she had spent most of her working hours for the last year or more? Different from Tony?

The aircraft had stopped, and the passengers were gathering luggage and coats. Marya retrieved her handbag from the floor and unbuckled her seatbelt. Craig was already on his feet. As the door opened, he gestured for her to precede him.

Conscious of his greater height, and far more aware of his body than she had been when they were sitting side by side, she slipped past him, nodded at the stewardess and marched down the corridor, her skirt swinging round her legs. She was not particularly surprised when he caught up with her, adjusting his long stride to fit her shorter one.

If she slowed down she would be holding up the passengers behind her. If she speeded up he would speed up too. Marya said testily, 'Is your wife meeting you?'

'I have never had the benefit of a wife, in Bergen or anywhere else,' he said smoothly.

'Very funny,' she snorted, and quelled an emotion that she refused to label relief.

'You can't be Norwegian, not with that red hair.'

'A direct descendant of Eric the Red.'

'I wouldn't be a bit surprised to find you had Viking genes,' he responded with considerable energy.

They had arrived at Customs. Craig was waved to the left, she to the right; by the time she had had her passport stamped, his bag was being inspected. She waited by the ramp for her suitcase to appear, knowing he would not be allowed to speak to her until her luggage was cleared, and saw him pick up his bag and then halt in frustration. Suddenly she was glad of the distance between them, glad that there would be no formal goodbyes. The sooner he left, the sooner she would forget him. For what was there to remember?

He raised one hand in salute and across the bare, high-ceilinged room called, 'Northwest Forestry...don't forget.' Then he turned on his heel and was gone.

With a squeal of metal the ramp started moving. Fighting a ridiculous urge to burst into tears, tears that she could not possibly justify, Marya waited for her suitcase, which to her relief was one of the first ones to appear. The Customs officer scarcely glanced at it. She passed through the frosted glass doors into the terminal, and no force on earth could have prevented her eyes from sweeping the area for a tall, tawny-haired man.

He was nowhere in sight.

CHAPTER TWO

FOR a moment Marya hesitated in the doorway, a sinking feeling in the pit of her stomach. An episode that had scarcely begun was over; and only now that it was over did she realise how astonishingly deep it had gone.

Just as well he's nowhere in sight, she told herself sternly. Just as well it's over before it began. You've got plenty on your mind without worrying about a man, Marya Hansen.

Clutching her case a little more tightly, she walked past a row of telephones and toilets, and turned the corner to find the counter for the Danish airline that flew to the Faroes. She saw their logo immediately. Standing below it, looking thoroughly out of sorts, was Craig Huntingdon.

Marya stopped dead in her tracks, and this time, instead of crying, could have burst into hysterical laughter. So much for his goodbye salute. So much for her last sight of him.

He was so wrapped up in an animated discussion with the uniformed ticket agent that he had not seen her; trying to stop her high heels from tapping too loudly on the floor, she walked up behind him and said clearly, 'Southeast Mining—right?'

His shoulders tensed. Very slowly he turned to face her, his grey eyes masked, his features expressionless. 'Northwest Forestry. As you well know. What are you doing here?'

'Going to the Faroes. Like you,' she said pertly.

'Not by this airline you're not.'

Her smile faded. 'What do you mean?'

'The fog's set in, and they have two planes stuck there already.'

Hoping against hope he was joking, certain he was not, she rattled off a question in rapid Danish and was given exactly the same information by the pretty brunette ticket agent. 'I was about to suggest that the gentleman take the ferry,' the young woman finished. 'The Norróna leaves at three. It would be better than waiting for an aircraft, I think.'

'Is the ferry fully booked?'

'I could check for you.' She picked up the telephone.

Marya switched back to English. 'Craig, the ferry is our best bet—if we can get on it. We'd be guaranteed of getting there tomorrow then.'

She had not noticed how naturally she had assumed they would be together. Without emphasis Craig asked, 'So you're going to take the ferry?'

The ticket agent interrupted cheerfully. 'I can reserve two tickets to Tórshavn. There are no cabins available, but there's been a cancellation and I could get you two couchettes.'

Quickly Marya relayed this information to Craig. 'I'm going to take it,' she said, and knew deep in her heart that she was glad the meeting with her father would be delayed by twenty-four hours. So her decision was really nothing to do with Craig, she added to herself. Nothing at all.

'I will, too.'

Once the agent had made their ferry reservations and issued them refunds for their airline tickets, Craig said, 'We haven't got much time—we'd better take a cab.'

They hurried out of the terminal and hailed a taxi; the driver put their luggage in the boot and Craig climbed in the back seat beside Marya. As they pulled out into the traffic he said edgily, 'I hope we're doing the right thing. We'll be a day late getting there—I hadn't expected that.'

For a moment he looked exceedingly grim. Marya said unsympathetically, 'If you're in a hurry, you're going to the wrong place. In the Faroes one goes with the fog and the winds and the tides—which no one can hurry.'

His eyes were trained on her face. 'It's your home, isn't it?'

'Yes.' She swallowed hard, trying to keep her voice under control. 'It's my home.'

'What's a couchette?'

Her head swung round, her eyes still full of distress. Blinking, she stumbled, 'A-a bunk. Why do you ask?'

'Like a berth on a train?'

So she was not to be allowed to wallow in homesickness. 'The ferry has cabins,' she said, 'but they're all booked, and anyway they're very expensive. So they have a number of rooms with twelve bunks per room, no pillows, no bedding, just mattresses. But it beats sitting up all night.'

'And the two we have are in the same room?'

'In the same room with ten other people,' she responded vigorously.

There was a gleam of mockery in the slate-grey eyes. 'I have a suggestion, Miss Marya Hansen.'

She had absolutely no idea what he was going to say. With all the hauteur at her command—and the restaurant had taught her quite a bit about hauteur—Marya said, 'I cannot imagine that anything you would suggest would interest me.'

'You haven't heard what it is yet.'

His smile, she had to admit, was well-nigh irresistible. 'You're much too sure of yourself,' she snapped.

The smile, if anything, deepened. 'We're going to spend the next twenty-four hours together...why don't we just relax and enjoy each other's company?'

'There's no need for us to even see each other again! There'll be dozens of people on the boat.'

'Why can't we spend some time together, Marya? It's no big deal.'

For some reason she disliked this cavalier attitude as much as his suggestion. 'I can think of any number of reasons,' she said.

'Spell them out for me.'

There was an edge to his smile now, a knife-blade edge that carried a warning. She said forcibly, 'They're none of your business—how often do I have to tell you that?'

'So you're a man-hater?'

She drew as far away from him as she could in the narrow seat; 'man-hater' was a word Tony had once flung at her. 'Do you play this game often? Make advances to a woman and when she declines—as she has every right to do—put the blame on her?'

He drew a deep breath. 'If that's what it sounded like, then I'm sorry. What I was trying to say was that although you're the most beautiful woman I've ever seen in my life, you've got a layer of ice around you, a "hands off", "no trespassing", "please keep away" sign...hence the label of man-hater.' He grimaced. 'Look at your hair, for goodness' sake!'

Thoroughly ruffled, Marya snapped. 'What's wrong with my hair?'

'It's a style that went out with the Victorian governess. Hair the colour of yours should be worn free.'

Emotions chased each other over Marya's face like wind over water. Then, a faraway look in her eyes, she said quietly, 'The fishermen in the Faroes have a saying—

do not let a red-haired woman cross your path, for she means danger.'

There was a small, tense silence. 'Are you warning me off?'

Marya shivered, for she would have said she had forgotten that saying, buried it deep under the concrete streets of Toronto. 'I—I don't know what I meant.'

'Why are you going home, Marya?'

'My reasons are personal,' she said with careful truth, staring down at her lap and trying very hard to keep any pain from her voice. 'But this I will tell you—I am not looking for a relationship. I don't want a man in my life. If that makes me a man-hater, then a man-hater I am.'

He said evenly, 'You don't feel that fate has thrown us together? After all, not everyone you meet in Toronto airport is going to the Faroe Islands.'

Her chameleon eyes, shadowed green, glanced over at him and darted away, for his soft-spoken persistence bothered her far more than his anger. 'That's just coincidence.'

'I'm not so sure.' The taxi screeched to a halt at some traffic-lights; they were approaching the docks. Craig added more urgently, 'We've certainly been thrown together for this ferry trip... at least give me the chance to get to know you better. The islands are big enough that we can lose each other once we land. If we still want to.'

Through the window to her left Marya could see the white superstructure of the car ferry towering over the dock. The last time she had seen it she and Tony had just disembarked, ready to set out on the next stage of their journey to Canada. Canada. Marriage. Happiness forever. What a fool she had been!

She said raggedly, 'No. There's no point in us getting to know each other. I don't want to.'

She began fumbling in her handbag to find her share of the taxi fare, so she missed the hardening of purpose in Craig's grey eyes and the angry tightening of his lips. But when she extracted a couple of notes a few moments later he rapped, 'What's that for?'

'My half of the fare!' she said in faint surprise.

Plainly she saw no need for discussion; she could not have known he was far more used to women who expected him to pay for everything. As he reached for his own wallet, Marya opened the car door and stepped out on the dock.

The sun was shining and on the breeze, conquering the stink of diesel and exhaust fumes, came elusively the crisp salt tang of the sea. She stood still, oblivious of the man who had joined her and of the eddying traffic, lifting her face, her whole body pierced with delight. She had missed the sea more than anything else, for it had been with her all her life, loved and respected.

'Here's your bag,' Craig said.

She glanced over at him, delight lingering in the curve of her mouth, her eyes still shining. He said roughly, 'You should look like that all the time.'

Reality returned with a rush. 'What do I have to do to get rid of you?' Marya demanded.

'You're a challenge,' he said lazily, heading for the ferry terminal. 'I'm used to women falling all over me.'

'So if I fall all over you, you'll run in the opposite direction?'

He grinned, the lines deepening at the corners of his eyes. 'I might. Then again, I might not.'

Her exasperated sigh was drowned in the roar of a passing fish truck, which left in its wake a very strong and quite unmistakable odour; again Marya stopped in her tracks, wrinkling her nose and suddenly laughing out loud. 'I'm going home!' she exclaimed, forgetting she wanted nothing to do with the man at her side. 'Oh, Craig, I'm going home...'

He struck a melodramatic pose and groaned, 'Forsaken for a fish truck.'

Her grin was impudent. 'Time you changed your cologne, perhaps? May I suggest Essence of Codfish—it drives me crazy.'

He said flatly, 'You're beautiful when you laugh.'

'I'm sure you say that to all your women,' Marya remarked. 'And now we'd better go inside and join the line-up... I did warn you about the line-up, didn't I?'

'I'm already learning to distrust that wide-eyed look of yours. You did not.'

She pushed open the door of the terminal, and saw that nothing had changed. The big waiting-room was crammed with travellers and luggage, the noise echoing from the roof. There were no signs indicating where anyone should stand, and no discernible organisation in the milling crowds; but the mood was clearly festive. Marya led the way to a mass of people on the left, put her bag on the floor and said, 'This is where we should be.'

Craig took up his stance beside her. 'The boat's supposed to leave in fifty-five minutes... we'll never make it.'

'Yes, we will. And no cracks about introducing any North American efficiency, either.'

'All right. But I do have to make a couple of phone calls.' He favoured her with a bland smile. 'Excuse me, would you mind keeping an eye on my bag?'

He could charm a herring from a seagull, Marya decided, and said sweetly, 'That's the second time you've used that line—you really do need to be more inventive in your approach.'

'This is neither the time nor the place,' was the even more bland reply. 'You're also beautiful when you blush, Marya Hansen... I'll be back in a few minutes.'

She watched him edge through the crowds, noticing how the women always gave him a second glance. She was as bad as the rest of them, she thought. Once they got on board she would ignore him. Pretend he didn't exist. She focused her attention on a rowdy group of young boys who were playing a cramped version of touch football in a small space to her left.

By the time Craig returned she and the bags had moved forward all of ten feet, at least thirty people were now behind her, and the game had attracted three more players and some good-natured protests from the crowd. Craig eased in beside her. 'It took all my inventiveness to figure out the Norwegian telephone system,' he said. 'I got cut off twice.'

Marya was trying to think of a suitably crushing reply when two of the boys tripped and were catapulted into the crowd, which fell back to give them room. Craig was knocked into her; to stop her from falling he put his arms hard around her.

She was thrust against his chest, off balance, and grabbed at his sweater for support. Her breasts were jammed into his ribs, and the rough wool grazed her cheek; briefly she was aware of the heavy beat of his heart, the strength of his arms and the dig of fingers into her back, before these isolated feelings were lost in an overwhelming surge of primitive desire. It was like an ambush, taking her completely by surprise, annihilating her normal control.

The body holding her was the body she wanted, craved, had to have, she thought helplessly. The body that had woken her from a three-year sleep...

Then, in the brief seconds before the crush of people eased, Marya felt his own arousal, and it was like a sheet of flame enveloping them both. The floor shuddered beneath her feet, and from a long distance away she wondered if she were going to faint. She, who had never fainted in her life.

Craig loosened his arms, drawing her up to face him. His eyes blazed into hers, his quickened breathing fanning her forehead. 'You felt it, too,' he rasped.

She was trembling as if she were in shock, and knew intuitively that what had happened, unheralded and unwanted though it might be, had in some way irrevocably changed her life. It was impossible to lie. She nodded mutely, her face pale, the gold flecks in her irises like tiny sparks.

Only when he pushed her away did she realise they were attracting attention by their very immobility; but when she raised one hand to tuck a stray strand of her hair behind her ear her fingers were unsteady, and she wished she had left the hair to trail down her neck. She could think of nothing to say, no way to bridge the immense gap between now and twenty seconds ago. Between what she had just experienced and the woman she had thought she was.

The queue moved ahead; she pushed her suitcase forward with the toe of her shoe and saw that the football players had melted into the crowd. Craig said in a voice pitched for her ears alone, 'Marya, I've never felt anything of that intensity in my entire life.'

She was agonisingly aware of how close he was standing, as if every nerve in her body was attuned to him with a sensitivity and precision she could not possibly escape. She had not, either. None of her dealings with Tony had prepared her for what had happened. Nor, even remotely, had the experimental kisses of her adolescence or of her rare dates in Toronto.

Craig said even more quietly, 'I told you fate meant to bring us together.'

She clapped her hands over her ears and said in a fierce whisper, 'It's not fate—it's sex.'

'Oh, there's more to it than that.'

'For you, maybe,' she cried in frantic repudiation.

'It was mutual, Marya—I saw your face.'

The queue was moving faster, although not nearly fast enough to suit Marya. She was suddenly flooded with terror, for she had had no control over her response, and control had been her god ever since Tony had left her, the one principle by which she had run her life. 'I don't want to talk to you any more,' she muttered, and tried to move ahead of him in the line.

He did not answer her. But neither did he leave her side. They shuffled forward in a tense silence, until finally it was Marya's turn at the ticket window. She explained in rapid Danish about their reservations and finished by asking, 'You wouldn't have a single couchette available in a different cabin, would you?'

'They're all booked, miss.'

Her face fell. She signed some travellers' cheques, was given her ticket and directed to another window to pick up a boarding pass. Without a backward look she scurried over to it, filled with the mad urge to run away from Craig and from the devastating discovery she had made in his arms.

But there was another, shorter queue at the second window, and a few moments later Craig joined her there. He said in a furious undertone, 'What did you ask the ticket agent?'

She turned to face him, her whole bearing full of defiance. 'I asked if any other bunks were available.'

'Good try. Do you always run away, Marya?' His gaze sharpened. 'Did you by any chance run away from home?'

In a bored, nasal voice the agent asked to see her ticket. Marya shoved it through the opening, was given a bright blue boarding card and began walking up the steps to the gangplank, not bothering to hurry, for Craig could easily catch up with her. As she stepped on the gangplank he said from behind her, 'It's a big ship but not big enough for you to avoid me for the next twenty-four hours. So why don't you stop running, Marya, and let's talk about what happened back there in the line-up?'

'There's nothing to say!'

A young woman in a red-striped uniform checked their passes as they embarked; Marya headed purposely through the scattered groups of passengers to the stairs that led to the sleeping quarters. She had a plan in mind: to change in the toilet into jeans and a sweater, do her hair differently, put on dark glasses and go up on deck. It was not much of a plan, but it was better than nothing. How could she talk to Craig about what had happened, when she could not begin to understand it and when it had scared her out of her wits?

She squeezed her way along the crowded corridors, checking the cabin numbers until she came to theirs. Pushing the curtain aside, she walked in. There were twelve bunks in two tiers, with two at the far end un-claimed, an upper and a lower; apart from luggage and sleeping-bags, the room was empty. She put her case on the lower bunk, for it would be easier for her to evade Craig if she didn't have to scale the metal ladders.

Craig flung his bag up on the top bunk and leaned against the ladder, a move which effectively blocked the narrow aisle between her and the door. 'So,' he said, 'we're alone—no small accomplishment on a ship this size. This might be an ideal time for the more inventive approach that you mentioned.'

Although his long body looked relaxed and there had been no discernible emotion in his voice, Marya was not deceived; there was purpose in the grey eyes and she already had an inkling of his physical strength. 'I don't want talk or action,' she said with admirable coolness. 'What happened back there was an aberration. It will not happen again.'

'How do we know if we don't try?'

He had straightened and taken a step towards her. Her back against the cold metal of the end wall, she said sharply, 'Craig, don't! I'll scream my head off if you as much as lay a finger on me.'

'That's a line straight out of a soap opera.'

Her eyes glittered. 'Then stop acting like the villain who has the helpless maiden in his clutches.'

'You look about as helpless as a wildcat.' He was angry, she could tell. But she was also beginning to discover he was a man who could contain his anger rather than acting it out. With a restless movement of his shoulders he moved away from her. 'You can't deny it happened.'

'I can make sure it doesn't happen again.'

'So you're a coward.'

'A coward for saying no to a man as used to having his own way as you?' she mocked. 'An innovator, surely?'

Unwilling amusement softened his face. 'You're different, Marya, I'll say that for you. And, since the idea of forcing myself on you doesn't appeal, I think a temporary retreat is in order—I need to consider my strategy. I concede the first round to you.' With a casual salute he added, 'See you later,' and left the cabin.

Not if I have my way, you won't, Marya vowed inwardly, and unlocked her case. She did not need to consider her strategy, for it was very simple: to prevent Craig Huntingdon from touching her ever again.

While she was changing in the toilet the ferry started moving, the power of the engines vibrating through the metal floor. She hurried back to the cabin, then headed for the sun deck to watch their departure. There was no sign of Craig. She tucked herself against the railing in the middle of a group of German tourists, and with a quickening of her heart saw the gap widen between the ship and the dock, gulls screaming above the churning grey-green wake. As warehouses and cargo ships fell away behind them, the seven mountains of Bergen glowed green in the sun.

The sea breeze teased her hair. Drunk with a happiness she had not felt for three years, she forgot about Craig and walked to the stern, a slim figure in well-fitting jeans and a bulky forest-green sweater, her thick braid tied with a patterned scarf. Beside her the Norwegian flag stirred lazily and below her the seabirds swooped in ever-widening circles. She was going home...

'I've booked a table for two in the restaurant for the second sitting,' Craig said.

So her disguise had been ineffectual; she had not really expected it would be otherwise. Marya looked up at him, one end of her scarf drifting across her face. 'You've met another woman already? How enterprising of you.'

He laughed outright. 'You underestimate yourself. It is not part of my strategy to find anyone else.'

In the sunlight there were gleams of gold in his thick hair; his face had strength and character more than conventional good looks, she decided thoughtfully, for his nose was slightly crooked and his mouth too wide. Sex appeal—he had more than his fair share of that. Not to mention confidence, and the casual, long-limbed grace of movement that she had to admit she found very attractive. 'I plan to eat in the cafeteria,' she said.

With a single swift movement he reached out and removed her sunglasses, holding them just out of her reach as she grabbed for them. 'That's better,' he said, 'I like to see the eyes of the person I'm talking to. We'll have breakfast in the cafeteria.'

Not for the first time, Marya found herself challenged by their clash of wills, all her senses stirred to life, the adrenalin coursing through her veins; she felt more alive than she had for three years. And she was quite safe— there was no risk of him touching her here on the crowded deck. 'I think the women in your life must have been a spineless bunch,' she observed. 'Or are you just naturally arrogant?'

'None of them was like you, certainly.' He grinned at her. 'Our table is by the window—you'll be able to watch the water while we eat.'

She raised her brows. 'Are you resorting to bribery? How very low-minded of you.'

'Nothing ventured, nothing gained.'

Abruptly, repartee changed to something else altogether. 'What are you hoping to gain, Craig?' Marya demanded, her face now openly hostile.

With all the force of his personality behind the words, he said, 'I can't answer that—because I don't know.'

Shaken, she said, 'You're honest, at least.'

'I promise I'll always give you nothing less than honesty, Marya. Back there in the shed you rocked my world. I still don't know how or why it happened . . . but I'm damned if I'm letting you vanish from my life without a fight.'

'"Always" is a word that has no meaning for us,' she flashed.

'We make our own meanings. Haven't you discovered that yet?'

Her accent getting stronger in her agitation, she retorted, 'We choose whether or not we wish to make meanings. One person cannot choose for two—haven't you discovered *that* yet?'

'Then I'll have to do my best to persuade you, won't I?'

Breathing hard, she choked, 'You're impossible!'

'Why did you run away from home, Marya?'

He had unerringly found the weakest point in her armour. She gave him a ferocious smile and said, 'I'll fall back on my standard response—none of your business.'

'A man,' he said levelly. 'It was a man, wasn't it?'

Suddenly she had had enough. She whirled to face the stern again, the wake blurring in front of her eyes. In his own way Craig was just as determined as Tony had been, for Tony had brooked no opposition until he had got her in his possession; and it was only then that he had lost interest. She would never repeat the mistake of confusing lust with love. Never!

'I'm sorry, Marya,' Craig said slowly. 'I didn't mean to make you cry.'

'I'm not!'

A note in his voice she had not heard before, he went on, 'I'd really like you to have dinner with me.'

'Only if I pay for my own,' she snapped, and then instantly wondered why she had given in so easily.

'You can pay for the whole dining-room if that's what it takes,' Craig said, with such evident relief that she knew he had not been as sure of the outcome as she had thought. 'Hold still,' he added, 'your mascara's smudged.'

Taking a handkerchief from his pocket he gently touched it to the corner of her eye, steadying her chin with his other hand; and as he did so, there flowed between them the same vibrant current of sexual tension that had leaped into life in the shed. Marya stood very still, fighting it back with every ounce of her will-power, yet somehow knowing that she was defeated before she started.

Craig dropped her chin with an abruptness that spoke volumes. 'So it wasn't just a one-time thing,' he said harshly. 'I should have known better than to think it was.'

'With all your experience.'

He looked at her as if he hated her. 'I've already told you what's between us is unique!'

Because every word he spoke only added to the terror she was feeling, she sneered, 'Unique until the next woman comes along.'

'You really are a man-hater, aren't you?'

'No! You admitted yourself that I'm different from the rest because I say no. If I'd fallen into your arms right away, you wouldn't be calling me unique.'

He took his time in replying. 'That's where you're wrong,' he said. 'It goes a lot deeper than a simple yes or no.'

Daunted by his certainty, she said coldly, 'We're beginning to attract attention. And the reason I came out here was to enjoy the scenery.'

'Then I'll meet you outside the dining-room at seven.' He passed back her sunglasses, being careful not to touch her, wheeled, and strode away across the deck.

Marya turned back to the railing, blind to her surroundings. Earlier she had seen Craig as a man of the outdoors, a man whose work had given him strengths she could admire. Now she was not so sure, for there was ruthless purpose behind every word he had spoken, and she was frightened by more than the passion that had flared between them. He himself frightened her. Simply by existing, he was a threat to her, a danger.

The ferry passed under a bridge. Houses were replaced by cottages, trees by shrubs, and grass by the bare rock of headlands and small islands. An orange and white pilot boat skimmed across the water towards them, nestled against the *Norróna*'s side while the pilot jumped aboard, then raced away. The deck began a slow, graceful rolling as they headed out to sea.

Many of the passengers had gone inside by now, for the wind had freshened, and the coast of Norway was dropping away at the stern. Marya stayed where she was, her legs adjusting automatically to the heave of the swell. The churn of the wake and the low grumble of the engines were hypnotic, and gradually all the tensions of the past few days began to seep away. Once she got home, she thought, her sister Kathrin would see reason—how could she fail to? Kathrin's rich Canadian boyfriend would go back home where he belonged. Marya's father would be so happy to see his errant daughter again that the past would be forgotten. And Aunt Grethe would, as always, welcome her with open arms.

As for Craig Huntingdon, she had allowed herself to become overwrought from a combination of tiredness, jet lag and anxiety. The man was nothing to her. She had been silly to react the way she had. Pacing to the starboard side to gaze out at the horizon, she decided she had had enough of jumping to his tune; she would eat dinner in the cafeteria by herself.

Pleased with her resolve, Marya leaned on her elbows on the rail and gave herself up to the rhythmic rise and fall of the sea.

CHAPTER THREE

MARYA stayed on deck for another hour, until she was lulled into the kind of peace she had almost forgotten existed. The Danish airline—and the Faroese fog—had done her an immense favour by granting her this respite, she thought happily when she finally headed for the cafeteria. It was a good start to her first holiday in three years.

Teenagers eddied around the video games, and the duty-free shop was crammed with people buying alcohol and perfumes. There was a long queue outside the cafeteria. Marya glanced at her watch in dismay. So much for her plan to be seated at one of the tables eating her meal by seven o'clock.

From his stance by the opposite wall, where he had been surveying the crowds, a tall, tawny-haired man began to walk towards her. When he was in earshot he said, 'It's a good thing I made a reservation in the dining-room, isn't it?'

Marya had seen him coming. She answered composedly, 'I wasn't planning on keeping it.'

'I thought you might not. That's why I've been hanging around here waiting for you.'

'You think of everything,' Marya remarked with an edge to her voice.

He was standing two feet away from her, making no move to touch her, his long body relaxed. With absolute clarity she remembered the hard curve of his ribcage against her arm and the heavy pounding of his heart under her cheek, and all her new-found serenity vanished. She said tightly, 'Why did you have to leave Toronto the same day as me, Craig Huntingdon? Why couldn't it have been a day earlier or a day later? Then we'd never have met.'

'We were meant to meet. You with your red hair that spells danger.'

Marya's stock of swear words was not large, and none of them seemed adequate to express the way she was feeling. 'Let's go and eat,' she said irritably.

The main dining-room stretched the width of the ship with windows on either side, and was graced with white linen tablecloths, a pleasant hum of conversation and a very generous buffet. Marya and Craig were shown to their table, and while Craig perused the wine list Marya studied their surroundings with a critical eye. After he had given his choice to the waiter Craig said with genuine amusement, 'You look like my schoolteacher when I passed in my homework late.'

'The carpet under the buffet needs vacuuming, the waiter had a spot on his cuff and at least three of the dishes on the buffet need replenishing,' she said crisply.

'I bet you work in a restaurant in Toronto.'

'I'm the hostess at La Roulade. Or I was until I quit,' she said. She was quite safe to tell him because she would not be going back.

'I've heard of La Roulade—you must be very good at your job.'

'I hated it,' Marya said with an air of discovery.

'Is that why you quit?'

Her face closed. 'No.'

'None of my business.'

The corners of her mouth tilted. 'You're learning.'

'How long have you been in Toronto?' he persisted.

'Three years.'

'Have you lived anywhere else in Canada?'

Marya shook her head. 'I haven't been outside Toronto.'

'You've never seen the east coast or the Rockies? Why didn't you travel at all, Marya?'

'No money,' she said succinctly.

'Your job must have paid well.'

'I'd been saving up to go to university.' And precious little of her savings would be left after this impetuous trip home to see Kathrin, she thought ruefully.

Craig was studying her face, his expression unreadable. 'Are you engaged? Or in any other way spoken for?'

With far more emphasis than the question called for, Marya said, 'I most certainly am not.'

'I see...so you followed a man out to Canada, he subsequently dropped out of the picture, you've been working at a job you hate so you can go to university, and I'd be willing to bet this is your first trip home since it all happened.'

His leisurely summary appalled her in its accuracy; all it had omitted was the series of waitressing positions she had held before La Roulade, some of which she preferred to forget, and her part-time job at the sports club. And, of course, her feelings. She stood up. 'Let's eat,' she said abruptly.

'He's the reason you're a man-hater.'

'He's certainly the reason I hate smooth-talking Canadians!' she said with absolute truth.

'I'll have to see what I can do to alter such a nationalistic bias.'

Marya stalked over to the heap of dinner plates, angry with herself for having revealed so much. But the array of food was very tempting, and the sea air had made her hungry; she took two pieces of pickled herring, daubed them with mustard sauce and reached for some smoked eel. When she and Craig were back at the table, he raised his wine glass in a toast and then began describing some of his travels to the Canadian Arctic and the Queen Charlotte Islands, his unforced love for his native country and his knowledge of its plants and animals kindling her interest. She asked a lot of questions; she told him about the puffins and oystercatchers of the Faroes; and she forgot that she hated smooth-talking Canadians. When they were ready to leave she said with artless surprise, 'I enjoyed myself.'

'I'm flattered,' Craig said wryly.

Nonplussed, Marya stopped in the corridor and gazed up at him: impossible though it seemed, she was almost sure she had hurt his feelings. Vulnerability under that air of confidence? Surely not. 'Do you streak your hair?' she said severely.

'No—the sun bleaches it. Do you dye yours?'

'Too expensive. Why are you going to the Faroes, Craig?'

He looked at her unsmilingly. 'I'm not ready to share that with you.'

'None of my business.' It was not a response she cared for when it was turned against herself.

'Right. Can I buy you a drink in the bar?'

'No, thanks—I'm going up on the deck,' she said. She gave him a quick smile, then hurried to the cabin to get her jacket before she could change her mind. He did not come after her.

By the time she had stationed herself at the railing, the North Sea oil rigs were vanishing beneath the horizon and the inshore gulls had been replaced by kittiwakes and fulmars and skuas, birds of the open sea. Craig Huntingdon was nothing to her. So why had she been tempted to sit in a smoky bar just to watch the play of expression in the deep-set grey eyes and the laughter

lines fan across his cheeks? Because he shared some of
her interests in a way Tony never had? Was that why?
But that was no reason to chase after him, and thereby
become one more woman in a long parade of women
who had fallen for his rugged good looks and his undoubted charm...

However, as Marya stood in her corner near the stern
the spell of the sea worked its magic once again, res-
toring the tranquillity she had felt earlier; Craig dropped
to the back of her mind. Every throb of the engines was
bringing her closer to home, to the family she had left
so precipitously three years ago, to the cliffs and hills
and tides of the island where she had grown up. She
owed Kathrin a debt of thanks, she thought soberly, for
if her sister had not fallen so disastrously in love, she,
Marya, would still be in Toronto, and the rift with her
father would be untended.

She stayed on deck until nearly eleven, by which time
the sky was washed with gold and the fulmars were
arched black silhouettes against a gilded sea. On the
middle deck she found a group of Faroese singers
chanting the old ballads; a couple of the singers recognised her, beckoning her to join them, and as she slipped
into a seat and picked up words she had known since
childhood, she was overcome with a flood of memories
as deep and swift as the tides around Risin and Kellingin,
the rocks that guarded the harbour at Tjørnuvík. She
did not see Craig watching her from a shadowed corner,
nor did she notice when he left. When she went to the
cabin past midnight, the top bunk over hers and her own
lower one were the only ones empty.

With a stab of an emotion she refused to call jealousy
Marya wondered if he had found a woman more agree-
able than herself. More willing. Frowning, she arranged
a heap of clothes as a pillow, took off her sneakers but

nothing else, and climbed into the lower bunk. Arranging her jacket over her legs, she turned her face to the wall and closed her eyes.

She must have fallen asleep right away, for when she woke she had the sense of having slept for some time. Across from her a man was snoring; he was a dedicated and inventive snorer, easily conquering the soothing grumble of the engines and the ceaseless rattle of metal. Her hands and feet were very cold.

She tried to cover more of herself with her jacket, and lay down again, in her mind tracing the narrow little streets of Tjørnuvík and counting its inhabitants one by one. The snorer gasped and snorted and sighed; she began to shiver.

Eventually she slipped out of the bunk, put her sneakers back on and went to the bathroom, where she held her hands under the tap in the hottest water she could stand. Her face, pinched and tired under its crown of chestnut hair, stared at her from the mirror. Would Kathrin think she had changed? Would Magnus, her father?

The mirror gave her no answers. After drying her hands, she padded back to the cabin. When she pushed the curtain aside to enter, a man was standing in the aisle. Craig.

He smiled at her in the semi-darkenss and whispered, 'I gave him a good poke.'

Realising that the snorer was silent, trying not to stare at the thin, tight T-shirt which, with his cords, was all Craig was wearing, Marya managed to smile back. 'Good for you.'

He stood aside to give her room. 'Are you all right?'

Startled, she muttered, 'I'm cold.'

He hesitated. 'Why don't we switch bunks? It's warmer up top. And I'll lend you my jacket.'

'But you'll need it.'

'I'm almost never cold.'

Anything would be better than standing six inches from the hard wall of his chest and knowing in her heart of hearts that she longed to touch him. To be warmed in the circle of his arms. 'Thanks,' she mumbled, and climbed the ladder with something less than grace.

'Lie down.'

Marya did as he asked, then felt him pull a down-filled jacket over her shoulders, adjusting it carefully to cover as much of her as he could. Then he took her jacket and spread it over her legs. 'There,' he said. 'That should be better.'

'Thank you,' she whispered, disarmed by his gentleness.

His face level with the mattress, Craig took his sweater from the bunk and pulled it over his head. 'Sleep well.' Then he disappeared from sight, and she heard the small sounds of him settling in her bunk.

He had not tried to touch her, or to take advantage of the situation in any way.

Marya lay very still. Her cheek was resting on what she thought was a pile of clean shirts, and from the folds of Craig's jacket she caught the clean, masculine scent of his body; huddling into its soft warmth seemed as intimate as holding the man himself. His head would now be cradled by two of her sweaters, and he himself would be lying where she had lain.

With shocking suddenness her body sprang to life, her breasts aching for his touch, her hips to be gathered in to the length of his thighs, the hardness of his passion. She buried her face in his jacket, terrified that somehow he would sense her response, yet certain in her very bones that he could match her, passion for passion, fierce in his desire.

She had subdued the tatters of her sexuality when Tony had left, and no one she had met since then had caused even a ripple in her self-control; it had taken a tawny-haired stranger to bring her to life again. She remembered her response in the shed in Bergen, a response she had not anticipated and could not possibly have quelled, and was afraid.

Screwing her eyes tight shut, she fought back images of the flame of her hair spread over his bare chest, of the intentness in the grey eyes were he to see her naked. She must not think this way, must not even imagine herself in bed with Craig. Although love, the innocent, trusting love of a young girl, had driven her into Tony's arms, she was honest enough to know now that the hungers of her body had played their part in keeping her there; but neither love nor desire had been enough to hold him.

She must not fall into that trap again.

Because she had not adjusted to Norwegian time, Marya slept late the next morning. Craig had gone, and her clothes had been neatly folded and put back in her case. She rebraided her hair in the bathroom, splashed cold water on her face, and went to the cafeteria for breakfast.

Although most people had eaten and gone, Craig was sitting by the window reading a book and sipping on a cup of coffee; he saw her immediately, and waved to her.

It would have been churlish to sit at any of the other tables. Marya headed towards him with her loaded tray, giving him a cautious smile as she sat down. 'Good morning,' she said.

'How did you sleep? Did you manage to get warm?'

She looked up to find his eyes intent upon her face, just as she had fantasised them. Flushing a brilliant scarlet, she dropped her gaze to her plate. 'Yes, thanks.'

'Marya, for God's sake—don't look at me like that in a public place,' he said in a strangled voice.

Her head jerked up, her mouth a hostile line. 'Like what?' she demanded.

'As if you've just been to bed with me.'

Heat coursed through her body. 'I don't understand you,' she choked. 'In the cabin last night when everyone else was asleep and it was dark you didn't as much as hint that there was anything on your mind other than my comfort. This morning in broad daylight in the cafeteria you talk about us being in bed together.'

Anger and frustration churned in the clouded grey of his eyes. 'I was fighting to keep my hands off you last night—didn't you realise that? Do you think it didn't occur to me how I could have kept you warm? Particularly after I'd got into your bunk, where all I could smell was your perfume.'

It did not seem to be the moment to tell him how she had reacted to being wrapped in his jacket. 'Oh,' she said.

'Anyway,' he added with an inimical smile, 'you must have made love in daylight before.'

Oddly enough, she had not. Tony had been a night-hawk, sleeping until well into the afternoon, then going out on the town until the small hours of the morning, dragging her from club to club and bar to bar; he had always wanted to make love at three a.m.

Craig let out his breath in a long sigh, stretching the tension from his neck. 'You have a very expressive face,' he said flatly. 'I would gather you haven't.'

'No, I haven't! One thing about you, conversations are rarely dull.'

'This man who hauled you off to Toronto, was he blind, impotent and half-witted?'

'Craig,' she said spiritedly, 'why don't you go and get yourself another cup of coffee? And take your time doing it.'

Although her cheeks had faded from scarlet to rose-pink, her eyes still glowed green. He said deliberately, 'What would have happened if we'd been put in a cabin together last night, Marya?'

'Nothing!'

'You don't believe that any more than I do. Deny that you were thinking about us making love last night.'

'Coffee, Craig,' she said through gritted teeth, the colour surging back into her face.

'You'd make a terrible liar. And a worse actress.' He picked up his cup and saucer. 'I trust you weren't thinking of studying drama at university?'

She looked him full in the eye. 'Biology,' she said gently. 'Perhaps you'd bring some jam for my toast, please?'

He stood up. 'And a steak knife or two? To defend your virtue?'

'A pepper shaker is much more effective.'

He laughed. 'I forgot you worked in a restaurant,' he said, and headed for the counter.

She watched over her shoulder as he threaded his way through the tables. One of the most dangerous things about Craig Huntingdon was the way he could read her mind...how had he known that she had been lying in his bunk aching to hold him in her arms?

Turning her attention back to her tray, Marya began carefully dissecting her grapefruit. The sooner she got off this ferry, the better.

As if she had spoken out loud, Craig said as he passed her two small plastic containers of jam, 'I have a rental car waiting for me at the dock—that was one of the phone calls I made before we left. I'll drive you to wherever you're going.'

'No, thank you,' Marya said politely, for he would then know exactly where she lived.

'It would be no trouble.'

'The bus is no trouble, either.'

'So you don't live in Tórshavn.'

The ferry landed in Tórshavn, the capital of the islands, named for the Norse god Thor. Marya put down her spoon. 'Craig, let's get something straight. OK, so my hormones start dancing all over the place whenever you come within six feet of me. That's all very nice, and if you want to feel flattered, by all means do. But I learned three years ago not to trust that particular dance. I will not have an affair with you. And anything else is out of the question, because you come from Vancouver and I come from the Faroes and five thousand miles is, even in the twentieth century, a slight impediment to a relationship.' She added cream to her coffee. 'Do I make myself clear?'

'Devastatingly so,' he drawled. 'You're afraid I'll find out where you live, that's why you don't want to drive with me. But there must be official birth records for the islands, and not that many females called Marya Hansen would have been born twenty or so years ago.'

'Twenty-two years.' Marya took a deep breath. 'Since you're so clever I'm sure you'd have no difficulty finding out where I live...after all, you could always play detective and follow the bus in your car.'

'That had occurred to me,' he said imperturbably. 'Me and Tom Selleck.'

'You're missing the point! If you turn up in my home village, the message will be the same—I don't want to see you, I want you to stop bothering me, I want you to leave me alone.' Viciously she ripped the foil cover off the jam container and stabbed her knife into the red, gluey strawberries. 'I'm not being coy or playing hard to get. I'm not playing games at all. I'm just not interested in spending any more time with you!'

'Not interested, or scared to death?' Craig said with icy precision.

Slathering far too much jam on her toast, Marya said haughtily, 'My reasons are my own concern.'

He reached over, took the knife from her fingers and snapped, 'I was brought up to look at the person I was speaking to.'

His fingers had been warm, searing her nerves. Her eyes flew up to meet his. 'Scared to death,' she said pithily.

He leaned back in his seat, holding her gaze with his. 'Ah...now we're getting somewhere. I like the way you operate, Marya Hansen—you look angry enough to poke my eyes out, yet at the same time you're honest.'

Tony had not wanted her honesty; had fled from it. She had, she realised with an unpleasant lurch in her stomach that did nothing for her appetite, underestimated Craig Huntingdon in assuming he would do the same. Craig relished her honesty, relished this battle of wills. Because it increased the challenge? With rather more restraint she said, 'Yes, you frighten me. Whatever it is that happens when we come within ten feet of each other frightens me. But I can make choices, Craig. I am choosing to pay attention to that fright. You must know the old biological maxim of fight or flight. I'm choosing flight.'

'Fighting's more fun. And in the long run more productive.'

'For you, maybe.'

Craig leaned forward. 'What in God's name did he do to you, this man who sweet-talked you to Toronto and then waved goodbye?'

He had left her alone, alone without money, in a city whose language was not her own, a city as alien to her as another planet, in a country where she did not know another soul. She had been nineteen years old...

With savage emphasis Craig said, 'I could kill him for bringing that look to your face.'

Marya gave a tiny, unconscious shudder; for a crazy moment she wished she could lean her cheek against Craig's broad chest, feel the strength of his arms around her, and cry her eyes out. She had been too shocked and numb right after Tony's departure to cry; and then the desperate, terrifying battle for survival had claimed her, and any tears had been buried deep in her psyche.

'He killed something in me,' she said in a low voice. 'Go away, Craig, and find someone else. Please.'

The jam-smeared toast wavered in her vision. Wondering dimly if she was going to be sick, she scrambled to her feet, muttered, 'Excuse me,' and fled from the cafeteria. She took the stairs to the upper deck two at a time and went into the first lavatory she came to; panting, she stared at her stricken face in the mirror and wondered which of the two men she had been running from; Craig or Tony.

Both of them, she decided miserably. The memories of Tony, memories she had never dealt with; and the fascination of Craig, the bodily pull, the clash of wills.

I don't want either of them, she thought. I want to stop Kathrin from making the same mistakes I did, and I want to make peace with my father. That's all.

It seemed more than enough.

Still breathing hard, she splashed cold water on her face and pulled open the heavy wooden door. The cor-

ridor was empty. Avoiding the area of their cabin, for
if Craig was looking for her that was where he would
start, she went down one flight of stairs and heard the
plangent singing of the group she had joined the night
before. She could take refuge among them, she thought,
glancing at her watch. The ferry would be arriving in
Tórshavn after lunch. All she had to do was keep away
from Craig for four more hours.

The group welcomed her in their midst, and soon her
pleasant soprano was following tunes that Aunt Grethe
had hummed at the spinning wheel and Magnus had
whistled in the boat-house. Fifteen minutes later Craig
entered the lounge; Marya saw him immediately, and
saw too that he instantly understood her strategy. His
shoulders tensed. Glad that she was tucked away at the
back of the group, she looked away and sang a little
louder—and knew in her bones when he left the room.

The singers stopped for lunch at noon, and Marya
allowed herself to be swept along with them to the cafeteria, chattering to her two acquaintances in Faroese,
the language gradually refamiliarising itself on her
tongue. She lingered as long as she could over her open-
faced sandwiches, but other passengers needed their
seats, and she wanted very much to be on deck when
land was sighted. Saying goodbye, she slipped out on to
the sun deck at the stern and peered over the railing.

On the horizon was a bank of fog, a shifting mass of
grey against the blue of the sky. Home, Marya thought,
and felt her heartbeat quicken.

'I figured you'd have to come out here sooner or later,'
said Craig.

He sounded extremely angry. She turned to face him,
noticing with one part of her brain that there were only
five other passengers on deck, all of them looking the
other way. 'I wish you'd take a hint,' she said coldly.

'I have,' he answered with a wolfish grin. 'I came out here to say goodbye.'

He was crowding her into a corner of the railing, his eyes hard with purpose. But as she opened her mouth to object, he took her in his arms, his big body blocking out the sun, and bent his head to kiss her. She made a tiny sound indicative of protest and panic, and then his lips were moving on her own with a gentleness that belied the steel grip of his embrace and took her completely by surprise. Her head began to swim.

Gentleness, yes. But also warmth and a confidence in his ability to please her. She tried with the last shred of her control to deny him that ability, stiffening her muscles in repudiation, clenching her fists to his chest. But the heat of his skin seeped through his sweater; her palms flattened, seeking the warmth of his taut flesh, her fingers without conscious volition sliding up his chest past the arch of collarbone to the breadth of his shoulders. When he drew her closer, the soft swell of her breasts rubbed against his body.

Overwhelmed by hungers as old as time, Marya kissed him back, and as if that were all the signal Craig had needed he teased her lips apart with his tongue and with one hand clasped her waist and drew her against the length of his body. She quivered from head to foot, for there could be no doubt that he wanted her, and the last shred of her resistance was engulfed in the primitive certainties of passion.

It was Craig who drew back, loosening his hold, dropping quick, light kisses on her cheeks and closed lids, murmuring into her ear, 'I chose the wrong place—they'll be throwing us into the brig if we keep this up.'

His voice was unsteady, and beneath her palms was the racing of his heart. Feeling as though she had travelled an immeasurable distance only to arrive back at her starting point, Marya opened her eyes.

The deck was still rolling easily in the swell, the sea and sky were a brilliant blue, and the fogbank lay on the horizon like a huge sleeping animal. She took a step back and saw, too, how Craig made no attempt to hold her against her will. He had done nothing against her will, she thought sickly. He had done nothing but call up in her a response he had known would be there. Waiting for him.

She said in despair, 'Why did you do that, Craig?'

'I thought I could kiss you and walk away,' he said hoarsely. 'Make you sorry for hiding from me. Make you change your mind.' He gave a sudden, caustic laugh. 'All I did was tighten the bonds you've wound around me, red-haired woman who spells danger.'

'I didn't mean to—I don't want to,' she whispered incoherently.

'Maybe not. But you want me in other ways, Marya.' His eyes bored into hers with all the strength of his will. 'Look, it shouldn't take long for me to do my business here. Then I'm free. Let me come and see you. I promise I won't pressure you into an affair, I won't even kiss you . . . but at least let's give each other a chance.'

The pulse was still throbbing at the base of Marya's throat and control had become a word without meaning. The bank of fog was closer now, its flanks shifting so that briefly there appeared a narrow line, darker than the mist, more substantial. Without warning her eyes filled with tears that clung to her lashes; one spilled on to her cheek and trickled to her chin. She raised her head, too proud to wipe it away. 'No,' she said. 'No.'

'You're a coward, Marya. A coward and a fool.'

Was she? Or was she instead using wisdom learned through experience to save herself from the pain of another rejection? Seeking out the spreading grey and white pattern of the mist on the horizon, she saw it had swallowed up that ephemeral glimpse of land as if the land did not exist.

'I don't think so,' she said steadily. 'Goodbye, Craig.'

A mixture of emotions chased each other across his face; the first, she was almost sure, had been a flash of pure agony. But before she could do anything it was gone, and he was saying with a formality that in no way masked an intense anger, 'You're making a mistake— you know that as well as I do. To be fully alive means to take risks, whereas by equating me with that other man, you're choosing the safe and narrow path...red hair can fade, Marya.'

She was suddenly afraid, for what if he were right? What if the tumult of emotion she felt in Craig's arms could be the harbinger of a happiness greater than any she had ever known? If that was so, then she truly was being a fool.

But three years ago on this very deck she had stood in the circle of Tony's embrace watching the mist-shrouded islands sink below the horizon and had thought herself to be happier than it was possible to be...the risk she had so blithely taken then had been the foolish one. Schooling her features to immobility, for she did not want Craig to guess her doubts, she said icily, 'I would not, of course, expect you to see it otherwise.'

'I see.' He gave her a curt nod. 'I've always hated protracted goodbyes...take care of yourself, Marya.' Then he pivoted, pulled open the cafeteria door and disappeared inside.

Marya turned back to the railing, gripping it with both hands as she fought back an almost unconquerable urge to run after him and fall into his arms. How could a man she had known less than two days be causing her such turmoil? It was ridiculous! Irrational, crazy, impossible. It was also, she acknowledged with a wry grimace, horribly painful to be so wrenched by doubts and fears.

She stared down at the water, where the foam hissed and seethed against the sides of the ship and the fulmars skimmed the surface on stiff wings. Puffins skittered away from them, wings flapping, red feet dangling, the light catching on their multicoloured beaks. Razorbills, more sedate, bobbed on the waves then dived out of sight with scarcely a splash. Then Marya looked up and saw the unmistakable solidity of land above the white swath of mist.

The land of maybe, she thought. But she had not said maybe. She had said no. And Craig had heard her; Craig would not be back. Goodbye to him would mean goodbye...

Tension caught her by the throat, and if Craig had walked up to her then she was sure she would have thrown herself at him regardless of the consequences. But he did not; and, although more and more passengers thronged on to the deck, he was not among them.

A crew member hoisted the white, red and blue Faroese flag. The puffins grew more numerous. The fog gathered them in, the air chill, salty and damp, taking Marya back to the little cove where she had grown up near a grey sand beach and the ceaseless roar of the tides. And then through a gap in the fog a ridged, humpbacked cliff topped with wet green grass came into view: the island of Nólsoy that sheltered the entrance to the harbour.

The harbour itself was free of mist, the ranked houses and sheds of Tórshavn clustered beneath the treeless hills reassuringly unchanged. From Tórshavn Marya would catch the bus that would take her home; once on the bus she would be hidden from Craig. She found herself praying she would not bump into him in the cabin or on the dock, for if she did she had no idea what she would say or do.

The *Norróna*'s whistle blasted, echoing back and forth as the gulls screamed in protest. With smooth efficiency the ferry nudged into the long wharf and the lines were dropped from her sides. On the dock people waved to relatives and friends, their upturned faces like pale saucers. Gathering her courage, Marya went below to get her bag.

The cabin was empty and Craig's luggage gone. She quickly applied some make-up, her original plan of arriving at her father's in her sophisticated summer suit no longer seeming very appropriate. Besides, the suit was thoroughly crumpled, having been slept on by both her and Craig. She bit her lip, briefly resting her forehead on the upper bunk, his steady grey eyes and broad shoulders as clear in her mind as if he were standing in front of her.

'You OK?'

She gaped at the speaker, a black-bearded young man who was hoisting a backpack from one of the lower berths. The dedicated snorer, she thought stupidly, and gulped, 'Thanks, yes—I'm fine.' She picked up her suitcase and hurried out into the corridor. Passengers swarmed around the exit to the gangplank, but none of the men had streaked blond hair over a sweater whose pattern Marya could have duplicated by heart.

Suddenly she could not bear the thought that she would never see Craig again. She wormed her way closer to the door, and when she finally emerged on to the gangplank, raked the dock from end to end. Then her heart skipped a beat. Beyond the Customs shed Craig was throwing his bag into the back of a small white car. Without a backward look, he climbed into the passenger seat and the driver edged into the stream of cars leaving the dock.

Her body sagged in bitter disappointment. Goodbye to Craig meant goodbye...she had known that. So why should she care that he had not even taken a moment to look back over his shoulder, to seek out one last glimpse of a red-haired woman among the throng of travellers?

CHAPTER FOUR

THREE hours later the blue and white bus turned the last corner and began the steep descent to the village of Tjørnuvík: the end of the road. Marya, who was the only passenger left, strained forward in her seat. In the curve of the bay at the foot of the mist-shrouded mountains she saw a little huddle of houses and the long finger of the wharf where she had played as a child. Then the river came into view, the walled fields of the *bøur*, that were so much richer a green than the *hagi*, the outfield, and the small circle of stones around the graveyard where her mother had been buried for seventeen years.

Her heart was thumping and her palms were damp with anticipation. The bus trip had plunged her into nostalgia, from every detail of the scenery to the cheerful greetings of the other passengers who lived along the route and whom she had known ever since she could remember. She was glad to be alone now, for she did not think she could have coped with small talk.

From the right-hand window the land dropped off sharply to an iron-grey sea; through the left she could see the pink blooms of ragged robin and the straggling gold of hawkweed poking through the long grass on the face of the cliff. The village grew closer, close enough to pick out a pony tethered near the riverbank, and the sheep that dotted the hills. Then, all too soon, the bus had pulled into the paved parking area near the beach.

'You're home again, Marya,' the driver called. 'How does it feel?'

'As though I've never been away,' she said, and knew her answer to be at least part of the truth. She hauled her bag off the overhead rack, smiled a goodbye and stepped down from the bus.

The church had been painted a fresh white. The potatoes were in bloom in Johan Olsen's little garden. Kristina Hansen, Marya's cousin, had a new car. But that was not surprising, thought Marya, for Kristina had the reputation for being the worst driver between Tjørnuvík and Tórshavn.

She was among the houses now, and saw the lace curtain move in Mrs Rasmussen's. So she was under surveillance, and the word of her return would soon be all around the village. And then her father's house was in front of her, with its tarred walls, whitewashed window-frames and turf roof. Behind it was the *hjallar*, the small slatted building where Magnus wind-cured his mutton, and behind that the shed where he built the boats that were his livelihood; a small thread of smoke drifted upwards from the stone chimney.

The house next door was Aunte Grethe's. The easy way would have been to go to her aunt's first, where she was sure of a welcome; steadily Marya walked towards the shed, pushed open the door and was instantly transported back to her childhood, for the air was redolent with the mingled odours of peat, wood shavings and her father's venerable pipe. Magnus Hansen was leaning over the gunwale fitting a rib near the bow of a sixteen-foot open boat, his knife in his hand, the black wool cap of a widower angled rakishly to one side of his head.

'Pa?' said Marya, and heard her voice as thin as a child's.

Only then did Magnus look up. 'So,' he said heavily. 'You have come home.'

'You don't seem very surprised...'

'I saw you coming through the window.'

But he had not bothered to come out and meet her. Marya said carefully, 'Aren't you pleased to see me?'

He put down his knife, took out his pipe and began tamping in shreds of tobacco. 'Have you brought the fine husband you went to Canada to get?'

Marya dropped her case with a thud. 'I wrote to you that there would be no marriage.'

His eyes, as pugnacious a blue as they had ever been, shifted to the stove. 'I did not read your letters.'

'Aunt Grethe must have told you. Or Kathrin.'

He pulled a box of matches from the pocket of his old wool jacket, lit the pipe and was enveloped in clouds of pungent smoke. He shrugged. 'Perhaps. Women's talk.'

Marya very slowly counted to ten. It would have been only too easy to slip back into the old patterns of her adolescence when she and her father had clashed daily, angry shouting-matches with neither of them backing down and nothing ever resolved. But she was twenty-two now, and had learned some hard lessons in the city that was so far from home. She pulled up a stool, perched on it and said, 'You were right three years ago when you warned me Tony wasn't trustworthy. Absolutely right. But I was too much in love to listen.' Magnus grunted. 'Then when he left me, I was too proud to come home.' She had also been too poor, but that was something she did not want to talk about.

'Why this visit, then?'

'I don't want Kathrin making the same mistake!'

'She was never as foolish and headstrong as you.'

All the old hurt surfaced in a flash. 'She was always your favourite—tell the truth.'

'And with good reason. I told you not to trust that Tony—but did you listen? No, you followed him to

Canada, and now you come back here with no husband and no wedding-ring, a disgrace to me in the eyes of the village.'

'You've never had any trouble holding your head up, Pa.'

Loftily he ignored her. 'Kathrin will marry her man, and he's a good man—she has chosen well. That's the difference between you.' Then his face darkened. 'Although a man from Eiði or Saksun, a Faroese man, should have been enough for either one of you.'

It was not the first time Marya had heard such sentiments. She said quietly, 'Tell me you're glad to see me, Pa.'

The fiery old eyes did not waver. 'I have work to do. Grethe will fall all over you if that's what you want.'

Marya's control vanished. 'I'm your daughter and you haven't seen me for three years!'

'Ah...' He gave a smug smile. 'I was wondering if you had changed, with your hair sleek as a seal pelt and your painted face...but you are the same.'

Magnus could needle her to anger as easily as the autumn rains could sweep down the hillside. 'You could at least make an effort to greet me.'

He balanced his knife in his palm and bent over the gunwale again. 'I didn't ask you to make a fool of yourself over some black-haired foreigner and follow him halfway round the world. And then stay there as though you had forgotten the land of your birth and the father who nurtured you.'

Aunt Grethe had done any nurturing there had been; but Magnus could always sweep the truth aside if it suited him. 'You're a cantankerous old man and I don't know why I love you,' Marya seethed.

The knife jabbed the smoothly carved rib. 'Go,' he growled. 'Before I ruin my hard work.'

'So boats are still more important to you than people. *You* haven't changed, either.'

'Go!'

Marya picked up her case and marched out of the shed, shutting the door with exaggerated care, not sure if she should laugh or cry. Magnus had always favoured Kathrin, and only Kathrin's loving and generous nature had saved Marya from resenting her sister. Whereas she, Marya, was like spark to Magnus's tinder.

She had never known why. She had rebelled against the arbitrary strictness of his rules and his lack of outward affection for as long as she could remember; now, for the first time, it occurred to her that perhaps this lack of affection could have been partly responsible for driving her into Tony's arms. And Craig's? whispered a little voice in her ear.

She did not want to think about Craig.

'Marya! Marya, you're home! Why didn't you tell us? I would have made apple cake.'

Aunt Grethe, plump and breathless, was scurrying down her back steps. She was not Marya's aunt at all, but a neighbour who had taken the two motherless girls under her wing seventeen years ago, looking after them in the day while Magnus had worked in the boat-house and returning them after supper to sleep in their father's house. Aunt Grethe had given them love rather than rules, gentling Marya's rebelliousness and fostering Kathrin's sunny nature; with her new vision Marya wondered what Grethe had gained in return. In a flash of intuition she thought Grethe, years ago, might have hoped Magnus would marry her.

Then she was gathered into a warm embrace against Grethe's starched white apron. Grethe's cheek still smelled sweetly of violets, and her eyes were the same soft brown as those of the eider chicks that bobbed on the waves in summer. 'You've lost weight,' Grethe scolded. 'And what have you done to your beautiful hair?'

'It's wonderful to see you,' Marya cried. 'You wrote me such lovely letters, you and Kathrin...they were my only tie with home.'

Grethe directed a dark look towards the shed. 'He wouldn't touch a pen to paper, not even when Kathrin begged him to. But he missed you, I know he did.'

Marya was not so sure. 'You're an incurable optimist who always thinks the best of everyone.'

'It's a good way to bring out the best in everyone,' Grethe said placidly. 'Come in now, and we'll make some tea and bake a cake for supper.'

'Where's Kathrin?'

Grethe nodded in the direction of the river. 'Up in the hills with her friend. She'll be home soon, I expect. Come in, come in...I can't believe you're home, so many times I've longed for this day.'

The kitchen was modern and as clean as a room could be, each one of Grethe's collection of china animals lovingly dusted, all her plants in bloom. 'What's he like?' Marya asked bluntly. 'This friend of Kathrin's.'

'Very handsome,' said Grethe, rolling her eyes. 'He thinks my fish stew is the best he's ever eaten.'

Knowing it was probably useless to ask for more pertinent information about the black-haired Robb, for Grethe had never seen beyond Tony's good looks, Marya remarked, 'She said in her last letter they were engaged.'

'He wants to marry her.' Grethe looked troubled. 'But she would be living in Canada, like you.'

He won't marry her, darling Aunt, thought Marya, and took down her favourite mug from the shelf. 'Once I've had my tea I'll walk up the river to meet them.'

'She'll be so happy to see you...she worried about you so far away. As for me,' Grethe scowled to the best of her ability, thumping the teapot on the counter, 'I've never understood why Tony didn't marry you. He loved you, anyone could see that. And he couldn't have found a finer match.'

'He wasn't the marrying kind,' Marya said fliply. 'Good-looking, charming, rich—and not to be trusted.' A perfect description of Robb, she finished inwardly.

'Maybe it was your temper,' Grethe added dubiously. 'You always did say what was on your mind.'

'I could have been as sweet-tempered as you and it wouldn't have made any difference.'

Although plainly unconvinced, Grethe busied herself making the tea and began chattering on about the neighbours and all the small changes that three years had brought. Marya listened with half an ear, glad of a respite. She would need her wits about her when she met Kathrin and Robb, for, despite the fact that she had travelled thousands of miles for this meeting, she had very little idea of how she was going to rout Robb and convince her sister to break her engagement.

One cup of tea and two raisin buns later Marya got up from the table. 'I'm going outside to see if Kathrin's coming,' she said, giving Grethe a hug on her way out. 'Won't be long.'

She wove through the houses to the road, hearing the rhythmic splash of the waves and the harsh calls of the black and white oystercatchers on the beach. The fog had lifted, so that patches of sunlight illuminated the grass high on the hills—a good omen, she thought, striding along until she had crossed the bridge. Then she cut up the trail parallel to the riverbank, where the burble of shallow water over the rocks drowned out the sigh of the sea. Leaning over the moss-covered wall that surrounded the graveyard, she found her mother's stone, and wondered, as she always had, what her mother had been like and whether she had loved the taciturn man she had married.

Raising her eyes to the vast, rock-strewn hillside, relishing the deep silence in which it lay, Marya idly searched for the moving figures of Kathrin and Robb; so soothing was the silence, so much an expression of all she had missed most in the noisy, dirty city streets, that her mission no longer seemed so important. She did not even miss the forests of Canada, she thought; the hills here, like all the land in the Faroes, were bare of trees, for the summers were too cold and short to support their growth, and the bones of the land were visible all year round.

A wren hopped along the top of the wall on the other side of the graveyard, and she watched it with total absorption. When it flew away, she wandered over to the chunky-bodied pony tethered out of reach of the potato plots and patted its nose, laughing as it blew into her fingers, hoping for a treat.

It was the pony who alerted Marya she was not alone, when it jerked nervously against her hand, the whites of its eyes showing. Its hoof struck a rock as it sidled away from her. Surprised, she glanced over her shoulder and her whole body tensed with shock. Craig was standing less than thirty feet away from her.

He said evenly, 'You're the last person I expected to find here.'

He was wearing the same sweater, and the wind was playing with his hair. That he should be here, in the village where she had grown up, filled Marya with such a confusion of emotions that all she could do was gasp, 'How did you know I was here?'

'I didn't. Oddly enough, I wasn't looking for you.'

Even then, she did not understand. Looking past him, she saw the little white car parked on the side of the road, and said accusingly, 'You saw me from the road. Who told you where I lived?'

'No one did,' he said grimly. 'The long hand of fate again. From Toronto to Tjørnuvík . . . I don't believe it. So this is where you live?'

She nodded dumbly, wondering with a superstitious chill how he had found her so quickly. Then she heard him say, even more grimly, 'Just why did you come home, Marya? Did you by any chance get a letter from your sister? Whose name is Kathrin?'

Her jaw dropped. 'Yes. How did you know?'

'Robb is my brother.'

With lightning speed the whole chain of events that had drawn them together fell into place. 'She wrote to me that she was engaged—that was why I came home,' Marya said dazedly. 'But she never mentioned Robb's last name . . . so it wasn't coincidence at all that we travelled together from Toronto to Tjørnuvík.'

'Although it might have been the hand of fate.' Craig had closed the gap between them, his eyes fastened to her face. 'So you came home to dance at her wedding—is that it?'

Too upset to be tactful, she cried, 'No! Of course not. I came home to stop it.'

'Come off it, Marya,' he retorted. 'Robb might be a young fool, but he's a damn good catch. Your little sister could have done a lot worse for herself.'

Her stomach lurched as another element of the truth tore at her composure. 'Robb is rich. Does that mean you're rich, too?' she whispered, and took an instinctive step away from him as though he might contaminate her.

'My father owns Northwest Forestry. News to you, Marya?'

The vision she had had of him striding along the forest trails in boots and a lumberman's jacket was replaced with shattering suddenness by the image of a man in a pin-striped suit sitting at a boardroom table. Son of the owner. A rich man.

In her first weeks as hostess at La Roulade Marya had attracted a certain amount of unwanted and unsought attention from some of the male guests, for she was both beautiful and unsure of herself in surroundings that were highly sophisticated. When in fury she had complained to the management, she had been told that she was on her own, and that under no circumstances must she upset the wealthy clients who were the bread and butter of the restaurant.

Money meant power; she had learned that very fast, and learned, too, to despise those who misused both. She overheard a great deal as she wove between the tables where the Bay Street executives made and destroyed fortunes and men. She knew which men were deceiving their wives and which women were high-class call girls, and somehow, over the fourteen months, all her anger against Tony had fastened itself on the rich men who came to the restaurant. She closed her eyes to the men of probity, to the men who always brought their wives and were unfailingly courteous to her, and saw only the others, the dishonest ones. The men who made deals. The men who changed women as easily as they changed their Gucci shoes. The men like Tony. The rich men.

And now Craig had become one of them. She said with utter loathing, 'Yes, it's news to me that your father owns the company. Do you think I'd have spent the time of day with you if I'd known the truth?'

His lashes flickered. 'Yes. As a matter of fact, I do.'

'Well, you're wrong! Tony was a rich man. Handsome, black-haired and rich—it could be a description of your precious brother, couldn't it? Do you think I'm going to stand by and let my sister throw herself away on a——'

A high-pitched call cut through her anger; the pony whickered. She turned and saw Kathrin running across the grass towards them, her head of tumbled curls yellow as a flower, her arms waving wildly. 'Marya—is it really you? Oh, Marya, you've come home!'

Behind her, more sedately, followed a black-haired man.

Then Kathrin had flung herself at her sister, tears streaming down her cheeks. 'Why didn't you let us know you were coming, it's so wonderful to see you, I've missed you so much...' Laughing and crying with the abandon so characteristic of all her emotions, she gave Marya a bone-cracking hug and then scrubbed away her tears with the back of her hand. 'I hate your hair like that,' she added decisively.

'If one more person remarks on my hair, I shall cut it off,' Marya said warmly. Then her eyes suddenly flooded with tears and her voice shook as she added, 'Oh, Kathrin, I missed you too—you don't know how much.'

'You should never have stayed away so long. I had to do my growing up without you.' Kathrin's face brightened, her smile like sun through mist. 'And guess what else I did—I fell in love!'

Marya's smile died. 'I know. I got your letter,' she said stiffly. Wishing she had rehearsed this scene which was so suddenly upon her—although no rehearsal would ever have included Craig's presence—she watched Kathrin whirl, her pretty blue skirt swirling around her legs, even her blonde curls seemingly in motion as her dazzling smile encompassed the man walking across the grass towards her. 'Robb, my sister's come home,' she cried. 'Isn't it wonderful? Now we won't have to wait until we're in Canada for you to meet her.' She seized the sleeve of his jacket, a dark blue jacket almost the same colour as his eyes. Guarded eyes, Marya noticed, that had taken in the silent figure of his brother without surprise.

Robb Huntingdon was certainly handsome, his features regular where Craig's were rugged, his hair black as a raven's wing and his body compact, without the loose-limbed grace of his brother's. As Kathrin laughed up at him, rubbing her flaxen head on his shoulder, her vivacity and sky-blue eyes were in charming contrast to his air of self-containment, and Marya realised sharply that in Robb she had an opponent far more dangerous than Tony. Tony had been all on the surface; this man, now giving her a sober smile, would keep his weapons hidden.

'Robb, this is Marya. Marya, Robb,' Kathrin chanted, as yet too caught up in her own happiness to be aware of undercurrents.

Marya did not offer to shake hands. 'Hello, Robb,' she said coolly.

He gave her a courtly little bow. 'Kathrin has often mentioned your name,' he said. Then his gaze drifted past her to the still figure of his brother, and he added drily, 'It would seem more introductions are in order...this is a regular family reunion. Kathrin, this is my brother Craig. Craig,' and there was now outright challenge in Robb's pleasant voice, 'my fiancée, Kathrin Hansen.'

With a rich chuckle Kathrin said, 'I'm still not used to being called that. How do you do, Craig? I'm very happy to meet you.'

Addressing his brother, Robb asked courteously, 'I expect you and Marya have already introduced yourselves?'

'Indeed,' Craig said.

'This is very strange,' Kathrin remarked, her head to one side. 'Both of you arriving at once.'

'I wrote to Craig, telling him I was engaged,' Robb said.

'And I had written to Marya!' Kathrin beamed impartially at the two of them. 'You both came to congratulate us—how lovely!'

'No, I didn't,' Marya began.

'Not quite,' said Craig.

Marya glared at Craig, ignoring the strength implicit in his features, seeing him as only one more rich man in the procession of rich men with whom she had come in contact at the restaurant and the club. Abandoning any attempt at finesse, she turned to her sister. 'Kathrin, don't you see? You're doing exactly what I did three years ago—making the same mistake. Robb won't marry you! He'll get you to Canada and once you've made love——'

She broke off, for her sister's red cheeks were an admission in themselves. With a scorching sideways look at Robb, she spat, 'He'll drop you. Why should he marry you when he can get what he wants without it? His kind doesn't bother with marriage. They take what they want and move on.'

The colour had faded from Kathrin's cheeks; aghast, she was staring at her sister. 'Marya, what are you saying?' she whispered. 'Have you gone mad?'

'It's you who's mad. He even *looks* like Tony!'

'He is *not* Tony, I told you that in my letter. Robb is steadfast and faithful in his heart—and of course we will marry. We love each other. Why would we not marry?'

Craig said evenly, 'I'll give you one good reason——'

'Stay out of this, Craig,' Robb warned, his fists bunching at his sides.

'Robb, you know better than to think I came here to congratulate you. You don't come into Mother's money until you're twenty-five, and even then I can get the lawyers to tie it up. Kathrin won't be nearly as keen on marriage to a poor man.'

There was a small, deathly silence, Marya's from shock and Robb's from fury. It was Kathrin who broke it, drawing herself to her full five feet five and saying with a dignity quite unlike her usual impetuosity, 'You are both wrong. Robb wishes to marry me, and I have no interest in his money.' Her face frozen, she looked from her sister to Craig and back again. 'I suppose I can understand why you are so bitter, Marya, although it is hard to forgive... as for you, Craig, I am surprised that a brother of Robb's could be so small-minded.'

Marya was struck dumb, for there had been scorn underlying Kathrin's even gaze, a depth of scorn that made her feel flayed; but Craig was patently unaffected. 'A million dollars isn't small,' he drawled.

In a stifled voice Robb said, 'I hadn't told her how much money was involved.'

'Sure,' was the derisive response.

As Robb took one step forward, Kathrin grabbed his sleeve, a sheen of tears in her eyes. 'Please, let's leave,' she begged. 'They're trying to poison what's between us, to make us as untrusting as they are—please, Robb.'

For a moment Marya thought Robb was going to disregard her; but then he looked down at her and saw her tears and said roughly, 'You're right—let's get out of here.' Putting his arm around her shoulders, he led her carefully around Marya and Craig.

Craig said calmly, 'I'm not finished, Robb. I'll see you later at the hotel.'

'You've done enough damage for one day—I don't care if I don't see you for the next week,' Robb retorted. Then as Kathrin tugged at his arm again, he turned his back on his brother and walked away.

Marya watched them go. She had a knot in her stomach, and all she could think of was that she had done a terrible thing. Her sister's shining happiness had been smashed; scorn and horror had risen in its place. And she, Marya, was at least partly responsible. Should she have waited until she and Kathrin were alone, instead of thrusting her views forward as soon as she met Robb? But that would have entailed the hypocrisy of false congratulations, of extending a welcome to Robb she could not possibly have meant.

I was right to do what I did, she thought frantically. I have to be right. Better that Kathrin be unhappy now, in the village that's home, than in a faraway land where she would be alone and defenceless.

But even as her brain was rationalising, her heart knew she would never forget what she had done. Nor, possibly, would her sister ever forgive her. She took a single, impulsive step after Kathrin, then halted in frustration.

'A penny for your thoughts,' Craig said.

He was standing with his hands in his pockets, watching her rather than the retreating couple, and if he was feeling any remorse he was not showing it. 'I'm not sure they're worth a penny,' Marya said in a low voice. 'They're not good thoughts—I hate myself for what I just did.'

'It had to be done.'

She could feel her temper rising. 'Maybe so. But they're people, not rocks on the beach—can't you show even a touch of emotion?'

'I don't like women who chase men for their money,' Craig replied, his eyes watchful on her face.

She said the one thing she was sure of in all this mess. 'Kathrin isn't the slightest bit interested in Robb's money.'

'She's a fool, then. Money makes a difference.'

'Do you think I don't know that?'

'You must have got money out of this Tony.'

'Oh, sure,' Marya said furiously. 'He paid for my ticket to Canada—a one-way ticket—filled the hotel room with flowers, and two weeks later left without paying the bill.'

'What kind of flowers? White roses?'

'You don't miss a trick, do you?'

His face softened with something that could have been compassion. 'White roses because you were a virgin.'

Her throat tight, she snapped, 'Stop feeling sorry for me! But do you begin to see why I won't allow Kathrin to make the same mistake?'

His anger was rising to match hers. 'Robb's young and credulous. But he's not irresponsible and he pays his bills.'

'All rich men are alike. Life's a game to them. They treat people like checkers, moving them around the board to suit their whim and, when they no longer serve a useful purpose, wiping them off without a qualm.'

'You're generalising, Marya.'

'I'm generalising on the basis of experience.'

'You can't say Robb's no good just because he's rich!'

'You can't say Kathrin's after his money just because she's a woman!'

Their voices had risen. Behind them the pony let out a piercing neigh.

Marya jumped, and with a touch of hysteria decided the pony's comment was as apt as any on all that had

passed. She said shakily, 'I'm going back to the house—
I've got to see Kathrin.'

'Going to give her your blessing, Marya?' Craig
taunted.

'No!'

He took her by the shoulders, his face only inches
from hers. 'You realise if this wedding takes place I'll
be your brother-in-law?'

She and Craig tied together, unable to disappear from
each other's lives: Marya felt a fierce surge of terror that
was inexplicably mixed with longing and said tonelessly,
'It won't take place.'

Then he was drawing her closer to his chest and she
knew what he intended to do. As her whole body sprang
to life, betraying her, treacherous as the currents that
swirled around the headland, she said raggedly and with
absolute truth, 'Craig, if you kiss me now, I shall burst
into tears—that's a promise. I don't cry often, but when
I do, watch out.'

'I'll risk it.'

She wrenched free of him and allowed some of the
anger she had been directing at herself to fly out at him.
'Or else I'll kick you,' she blazed, her eyes green as the
grass. 'As hard as that pony. None of your fancy
Canadian thoroughbreds can kick like a Faroese pony.'

The pony was dancing at the end of its rope, tossing
its head and rolling its eyes. Craig said levelly, 'With a
million dollars at stake I'd have thought a kiss might
have been good strategy.'

She glowered at him, some of the pony's wildness in
her mien. 'We're not getting into that again! Take your
brother back to Vancouver, Craig, where everyone bows
low at the name of Northwest Forestry and the women
are willing. Five minutes from now wouldn't be too
soon.'

She began tramping across the grass towards the bridge and heard Craig murmur close behind her, 'You have a nasty tongue on you, Marya.'

She increased her step. 'Go *away*.'

'I must say I never guessed you were the estimable Kathrin's sister. Robb wrote me a letter extolling her charms in quite embarrassing detail but neglecting to mention where she lived or her surname. Her financial status, of course, I took for granted.'

Marya's steps faltered. For a moment she saw the walled pastures, the tiny gardens and the little huddle of houses cupped by the bleak hills as an outsider might see them. A rich outsider. Like a fury she turned on him. 'Let me tell you something, Craig Huntingdon—something I learned at great cost in the prosperous city of Toronto. The people here *are* rich! Rich in a way you'll never know. They have a place in the world and work to do and traditions to nurture them—so stop waving your wonderful dollars under my nose, I don't want them any more than Kathrin does!'

'I don't believe you,' he snarled.

Now that she knew he was rich, she would not have expected a response any different. The splash of the river loud in her ears, she said softly, more to herself than to him, 'How strange...that I had to come back here to understand that about the village. All I wanted to do was get out of here when I was a teenager.'

'And will you stay here now?' Craig said harshly. 'For the rest of your life? It's a safe place, Marya.'

Craig, Kathrin, Robb, Magnus, Grethe...their faces danced in Marya's head, mocking and confusing her, each of them wanting her to behave in a certain way. And she, caught in their differing expectations, did not know what she wanted for herself.

The first step, she thought desperately, was to escape from the steel-eyed man in front of her. 'I've got to go,' she said. 'I have to find Kathrin and try to make her understand.'

Craig made no move to stop her. 'I'm sure I'll be seeing you in the near future,' he said ironically. 'Should you need me, I'm staying in the hotel in Eiði.'

Marya had met Tony at the hotel in Eiði the summer she had worked there as a waitress. With a small choked sound she spun on her heel and ran for the shelter of the houses.

CHAPTER FIVE

AUNT GRETHE was up to her wrists in bread dough when Marya rushed in the door. 'Have you seen Kathrin?' Marya demanded.

A small cloud of flour rose in the air. 'She ran in here, said she and Robb wouldn't be home for supper and ran out again. She had been crying.' Grethe gave an audible and disapproving sniff. 'Strange goings-on for someone whose sister has just come home.'

'Did she go over to Pa's?'

'She and Robb left in Robb's car. He didn't even come in, and I'd made fish pie specially for him.'

Marya sat down with a bump on the nearest chair. 'We had a terrible fight,' she confessed.

'You might have given yourself the time to get to know her young man before you decided he was no good.' Grethe gave the dough one last vicious thump and covered it with a cloth.

'It won't work! He lives too far away.'

'Your mother and father came from the same village and their marriage was as stormy as the weather in February.'

For a moment Marya forgot about Kathrin. Intrigued, she said, 'How do you mean?'

'Never mind what I mean.' Grethe bent down and took some potatoes from a sack by the sink and started to peel them, the knife flashing. 'I think it's a bad way for you to come home, Marya, so full of bitterness and anger. Sister against sister... what kind of a greeting is that?'

Marya had no answer, for the scene with Kathrin had torn her apart. Needing to be occupied, she began to lay the table. An hour later she, Grethe and Magnus ate the fish pie in a silence full of things unsaid, and afterwards she walked up-river to the waterfall where the spotted orchids always flowered in July.

Sitting down on a rock, she gazed out over the crescent-shaped beach and the enclosing cliffs, whose southern flank ended in the two sharp-pointed rocks known as Risin and Kellingin, the Witch and the Giant. She was the one who had behaved like a witch, Marya thought miserably. But how could she have acted any differently? Because she had travelled thousands of miles to protect her sister from another Tony, that horrible scene by the river had been inevitable.

It was only now, when she was alone, that she could acknowledge to herself the other facet of that scene: the realisation that Craig came from the same milieu as the clients of La Roulade. The strength in his face she now saw as ruthlessness, and what she had called self-confidence was instead the inbred arrogance of a man who had never had to worry about money or social position. Or women. He had been quite straightforward about that. She, Marya, had only interested him because she paid for her own taxi fare and declined to give him her address.

She leaned forward, riffling the grass with her fingers, tracing the layered pink and red petals of the orchids. Craig was rich. He was all that she hated most.

Blind to the orchids' beauty, she hugged her arms around her chest. Ever since Craig had left her down by the bridge the pain of this discovery had been lying in wait for her, a pain that overrode even the misery of her quarrel with Kathrin. The passion she had felt in his arms and the pleasure she had taken in his company had become cruel reminders of her gullibility. She had been, she thought dazedly, in danger of falling in love with him. Of doing just what she was warning Kathrin against. Had she learned nothing in three years?

If she saw Craig again, she must ignore him. Certainly she must never let him touch her again.

Marya went to bed that night in the room under the eaves in her father's house, the room she had always shared with Kathrin; but in the morning Kathrin's bed had not been slept in.

With a cold pang of fear Marya wondered if Kathrin and Robb had eloped; driven to Vágar and taken the first flight to Europe. Surely Craig wouldn't have let that happen. He, for all the wrong reasons, wanted this marriage no more than she did.

But Grethe, still looking aggrieved, explained that Kathrin had spent the night on the couch at her house, and had now gone to work. 'She works at a youth camp—you hadn't even found that out, had you?' she snorted. 'Hadn't bothered to ask.'

Aunt Grethe rarely lost her temper, but when she did the results tended to linger. Marya went outdoors, talked to the men who were up by the pens shearing some sheep, went for another long walk, and helped Grethe make rhubarb conserve. At eight o'clock that night she went back to her father's. Magnus was still in the shed, taking advantage of the long hours of daylight; she perched on her bed and tried to read.

Grethe disapproved of her behaviour. Magnus did not seem to care whether she was home or not. Kathrin was avoiding her. And, last but by no means least, Craig had become just another Tony.

Craig . . . she remembered the easy grace with which he moved, the shock of being pulled against his body, the intimacy of his kiss and the heat of her response. What did it all mean? He was nothing to her, nothing. Worse than nothing—for he was rich and she hated rich men.

Perhaps, she thought with another stab of the terror that always seemed to be lying in wait for her these days, he had already gone back to Canada with Robb, removing his brother from the clutches of a young woman he saw as money-mad. It would be a reasonable thing for him to do. And why would he bother to say goodbye to her, Marya? They had clashed ever since they had first spoken to each other.

Her hands were shaking. She looked at them dispassionately. The best thing that could happen would be for Craig to return to Canada without seeing her again. So why did she have this mad urge to borrow a car and drive to the hotel to see if Craig and Robb had checked out?

What if they have, Marya? What then?

An inner voice answered her own question. Your sister's heart will be broken. For which you must bear at least half of the blame.

And what of your heart, Marya? Will it be broken, too?

Unable to bear her own thoughts, she flung the book aside and paced up and down the bedroom. Then she went downstairs and scrubbed out Magnus's sink and polished the surface of the old potbellied stove until she could see her face in it. Beautiful, Craig had called her. But had he meant it? And would he have left without saying goodbye? Leaving her nothing but the name of a forestry company thousands of miles away as a clue to his whereabouts? The company his father owned.

Outside her father's house a car door slammed and then footsteps climbed the stairs. Marya clutched the blackened cloth, her heartbeat echoing in her ears.

Kathrin came in the door; she was smiling, a soft, glowing smile that Marya had never seen before. But then she caught sight of her sister bending over the stove and her face closed. 'Hello,' she said in an unfriendly voice.

Marya had dropped the cloth, her face drained of colour. Kathrin added sharply, 'What's the matter?'

'I thought you were Craig,' Marya blurted.

'Oh, he's back at the hotel, waiting to pounce on Robb and convince him I'm in love with his money,' Kathrin said bitterly.

Marya picked up the cloth, carefully folding it into a neat rectangle. 'You're not. I know you're not.'

'Tell that to Craig.'

'I did.'

'He obviously didn't listen. I don't know what's wrong with the two of you! Particularly you.'

'I want what's best for you!'

'Robb is who I want.'

'Kathrin, I thought I wanted Tony—and look what happened.'

Kathrin tossed her blonde curls. 'I can see exactly what's happened to you while you've been away—you've become so bitter and warped you don't believe any man is to be trusted, and if he happens to have money and black hair, then he's doubly condemned. Robb is *not* Tony, Marya—I wish I could convince you of that.'

Marya looked her sister squarely in the eye, and no force on earth could have prevented the words spilling from her lips. 'You listen to me for a while! I've never told anyone else what it was like three years ago, Kathrin. You know how strictly we were brought up—I couldn't make love without being married. So Tony lured me to Canada promising to marry me. I could have a dozen bridesmaids and a church wedding if that's what I wanted, a honeymoon in the Bahamas, new clothes, all the excitement of a big city—he didn't leave out a single temptation. And I fell for it. I was only nineteen, remember—just your age—and for months I had wanted to leave the islands. When we arrived in Toronto Tony booked us into this luxurious hotel and filled the room with flowers and then set out to seduce me.'

Staring out of the window, her voice emotionless, she went on, 'Pa was a long way away and I loved Tony, so I fell for that, too.' She shrugged. 'We stayed in that room for nearly two weeks, and gradually the real Tony emerged. Selfish, always craving new excitement and new thrills, unable to be alone or quiet. I wanted to go walking in the country and he wanted to be seen in all the right nightspots.' Another shrug. 'Very soon he let it be known the new thrills included new women, and that I really wasn't as interesting in that department as he had thought I would be. As for marriage, surely I hadn't been so unsophisticated to believe he was serious?'

Her face full of strain, she looked over at her sister. 'He waited to show his true colours until he was over there where he belonged. He never had any intention of marrying me, Kathrin—and when he was done with me he threw me aside like a pair of old shoes.'

Swiftly Kathrin crossed the room, putting her arms around her sister. 'It must have been terrible for you, Marya! Why didn't you come home?'

'I didn't have the money. I was too proud to ask you for it and too stubborn to ask Pa.'

'So instead you sent us chirpy little letters pretending everything was just wonderful.'

With passionate intensity Marya said, 'Kathrin, please don't make the same mistake I did.'

Kathrin's arms fell to her sides. 'I understand better now why you were so upset yesterday when you met Robb. But you've got to let go of the past, Marya. For your sake and for mine. Robb isn't Tony. He's faithful and true and kind, and he wouldn't change even if we went to the North Pole.'

'But he'll——'

'Craig is threatening to cut off Robb's money. That hasn't changed Robb's mind or mine. Drop it, Marya.'

'You'll regret it—I know you will!'

Kathrin said flatly, 'I'm going to sleep at Grethe's again. I don't like what you've become, Marya—you won't even give Robb a chance.' Her mouth, that smiled so readily, was a thin line. When she went out, she slammed the door as loudly as she could.

Marya went upstairs, but it was a long time before she fell asleep.

When Marya got up the next morning and peered through the small panes of the bedroom window she saw Magnus crossing the yard to the boat-house. She felt as tired as if she had spent the night following Tony from nightclub to nightclub; but the sun was shining and Kathrin had not left the islands with Robb.

She'd better do her best to prevent them from doing so, she thought ruefully, for if Kathrin and Robb got married Craig would be her brother-in-law. She had great difficulty picturing Craig in any kind of brotherly role. Only because he was rich, of course.

She pulled a hideous face at herself in the glass and went downstairs to have a bath. Although this entailed heating water and pouring it into the old porcelain tub in the little room off the kitchen, and she could have had a bath much more easily at Grethe's, she did not want to start her day with further doses of disapproval. Kathrin had spent a second night on Grethe's sofa, and Grethe would want to know why. Later, thought Marya, hefting the bucket off the stove.

The tub was too short, and she banged her knee getting out; but the hot water had done wonders for her morale. She scrubbed at her hair with a towel, noticing in the cracked little mirror how it was, as usual, a tangle of long red curls when it was wet. Then, over the gurgle of water in the drain, she heard a tap at the door.

Robb, she thought, come looking for Kathrin. Frantically trying to rehearse what she would say to him, she pulled on the robe that Kathrin had made for her last Christmas: smoke-grey cotton fashioned like a monk's cassock. Padding on bare feet across the floor, she pulled the door open.

The sun struck her in the eyes, glinting in her tumbled red hair, outlining her body under the long grey robe. 'My God,' said Craig.

With a gasp of dismay Marya stepped back into the shade and threw her weight on the door. But Craig was too quick for her. He inserted his foot in the gap and pushed hard against the whitewashed planks, so hard that Marya staggered backwards. Carried forward by his own momentum, he burst into the room. He then closed the door behind him and leaned against the rough, heavy planks.

Marya's face was pink with fury; because her skin was not quite dry, the cotton robe was clinging to her body at breast and hip. 'You've seen too many Rambo movies,' she snapped. 'Where's your machine gun?'

'Marya,' he said thickly. 'Marya, you're so beautiful.'

She could have run for the little bathroom and locked the door. But the pride that had sustained her that first long winter in Toronto kept her where she was: pride, and perhaps a remnant of the rebellion that Magnus had never been able to eradicate. She regarded Craig in silence, her eyes green with emotion, her chin tilted.

He was wearing beige bush trousers and a loose-fitting shirt, open at the neck, sleeves rolled up to the elbows; the look in his eyes made her tremble inwardly. Her hardened nipples thrust against the fabric, and the colour in her cheeks deepened.

'I don't even have to touch you, do I?' he said.

Hating him for saying what was so obviously the truth, hating her own body for betraying her so blatantly, she raised her chin a little higher and said nothing.

Then he took a step towards her. Marya held her ground, although her breathing quickened. Speaking with a deliberation that caught at her throat, Craig said, 'Marya, I know we've fought over almost everything since we've met, and that we certainly don't see eye to eye on the subject of your sister—but I want you to know I have never desired a woman as I desire you. Never. You're more beautiful than anyone I've ever known. That's the absolute truth, and I can only ask you to accept it as such.'

She scowled at him. 'Oh, I believe you,' she said.

'What? No argument?'

She remembered the abortive arguments with her sister and said drily, 'I think I may give up arguing—it's got me into nothing but trouble the last three or four days.'

Craig took another step towards her. As she waited with tightened nerves for whatever he would do next, she realised with a bewildering jolt that at a certain rudimentary level she trusted him. Right now he was being honest in a way Tony had never been, for Craig was not dressing up his desire for her as anything other than what it was: a passionate need for her body. He was not mouthing insincere words of love. He was not holding out false promises of marriage, lures to get her into his bed. He was simply saying that he wanted her.

He was now standing only six inches away from her. He stretched out one hand and touched her hair, letting a flame-red strand sift through his fingers. Then with both hands he lifted the mass of damp curls off her neck, holding their weight as if it were precious gold. 'Whenever you're with me, will you wear your hair like this? Loose, free to blow in the wind...'

On the hillside the day before yesterday she had resolved never to see him again. It had been, Marya thought wildly, an easy resolve to make when he was nowhere near her. 'There's no need for us to be together. Ever again,' she said forcefully.

'Oh, we'll be together, there's no question of that...please, Marya? Because by leaving your hair free, you're casting off those years in Toronto and becoming yourself again, the woman you were meant to be.'

And what kind of woman was that? The rebel, the fighter of her adolescence? The impetuous young woman who had crossed an ocean for love of a man? Or the efficient, hard-working woman she had become in Toronto, with rebellion and sexuality both firmly under control? She said, 'What I become is, to use a phrase you've heard before, none of your business.'

'Both of us deserve better than that.'

'Oh, deserve,' she said impatiently. 'My father, I'm sure, would say I deserved everything that happened to me in Toronto.'

'And Robb would no doubt say I deserved to meet a woman as stubborn and uncooperative as you.' Craig suddenly gave her a smile that took her breath away. 'Let's leave that word alone. As far as I'm concerned,

I haven't in any sense earned you—you're a gift, Marya. A quite wonderful and unexpected gift.'

Mesmerised by his smile, she stood very still. He let her hair fall, resting his hands on her shoulders and leaning forward to kiss her, and although she knew what he was about to do she was helpless to prevent it. The first touch of his lips was tentative, almost as if he were afraid of her. It was a long, slow kiss that throbbed through her veins; she was achingly conscious of her nakedness under the grey robe, of every brush of cotton against her skin. When he released her, there were points of fire in his eyes. Locking her gaze with his, he deliberately laid his palm on the swell of her breast. 'I can feel your heart beating,' he said huskily.

From the warmth of his palm sweetness flooded Marya's body and was faithfully reflected in her grey-green eyes. Unconsciously she swayed towards him. He stroked her breast from base to tip once, then again, his fingers lingering on the softness of her flesh. She closed her eyes, lost to everything but the pulse of desire radiating from his fingertips.

This time when Craig kissed her his mouth made demands, demands she was more than willing to meet. His arms went around her, straining her to his body, his hands searching out the contours of her flesh through the cotton robe. The pounding of his heart found its echo in her blood; she linked her fingers behind his head, her long sleeves falling back to her elbows, and felt his hands bury themselves in the heavy fall of her hair.

Time lost its relevance; Marya forgot where she was, and why, in the immediacy of the physical: the man in whose arms she was discovering such bliss. When he finally drew away from her, his lips leaving a trail of kisses along her jaw, his hands coming to rest on her shoulders, she gazed up at him with pleasure-dazed eyes and whispered, 'Why did you stop?'

Visibly struggling to control his breathing, Craig said, 'I could make love to you on the floor, you know that as well as I do. But this is your father's house, and your aunt lives next door, and either one could walk in at any minute.'

Marya's face clouded and a little of the tumult in her body subsided; along with everything else, she had forgotten about her family. 'But Kathrin won't walk in,' she said unhappily. 'She's not on speaking terms with me.'

'At about midnight last night Robb suggested I go straight back to Vancouver where I belong and leave him alone. Except that he didn't phrase it nearly so politely.'

'And are you going to?' Marya demanded, too overwrought to hold back the question.

'No.' He added harshly, 'Although as far as you're concerned, that would be the smartest move I could make.'

Her chin snapped up. 'Please don't stay on my account!'

'You're arguing again, Marya.'

'It's called sublimation,' she retorted with angry accuracy. 'We could go climb a mountain. Or jump in the sea.'

From the beginning, she thought fatalistically, she had loved the way the laughter lines fanned from the corners of his eyes. 'The temperature of the water down at the beach never gets much above five degrees centigrade—I'd suggest the mountain.'

He allowed his eyes to wander over the soft curve of her lips. 'But I might be tempted to make love to you halfway up.'

'You would wait that long?' she queried gently.

He laughed. 'Probably not. Nor, perhaps, would you.' As she blushed, he added with sudden intensity, 'There must have been men since Tony.'

She shook her head violently, the silken waves of her hair falling across her cheek. 'None!'

There could be no mistaking her sincerity. Craig said with suppressed violence, 'I have no right to be glad—but I am. Which is neither rational nor wise, and nothing whatsoever to do with the reason I came here in the first place.'

Obediently she said, 'Why did you come here, Craig?'

'To suggest we join forces to stop this marriage between your sister and my brother.'

Marya gaped at him in utter surprise and said coldly, 'How can we? When our reasons are so opposed? You think my sister's mercenary and calculating——'

'And you think my brother's a liar.'

'Not a very good basis for a partnership.'

'They've gone to Viđoy for a picnic,' he said abruptly. 'I figure she'll do her best to get pregnant—then he'll have to marry her.'

'How dare you even suggest such a thing?' Marya cried. 'Kathrin isn't like that—cold-blooded and calculating. Besides,' she added venomously, 'I'm quite sure your precious brother is experienced enough to avoid any unwanted consequences to his actions.'

'He's not experienced! That's what I'm trying to get through your thick head.'

'A partnership?' Marya repeated with heavy irony. 'You've got to be crazy.'

He looked as angry as she. 'Forget the reasons! Neither of us wants them to marry—right?'

'Right!'

'Then let's go to Viđoy. We might at least stop them from making love on the hillside.'

'Spy on them, you mean?' Marya said with evident distaste.

'Maybe they haven't gone there to make love. Maybe they're making arrangements to get married there.'

Marya paled. Kathrin had always loved the island of Viðoy, and in particular the village of Viðareiði, northernmost village in the Faroes; to get married there would be just the sort of gesture she would see as romantic.

'Come on,' Craig urged. 'I can see by your——' He broke off, for heavy footsteps were climbing the outside stairs, and then the door swung open. Magnus stepped inside.

He looked from Craig to his daughter, with her tousled red curls and her floor-length robe, and his mouth tightened. In his heavily accented English he said, 'You have not changed much, Marya. Home two days and already you have a man in the house.'

She flinched. 'Don't, Pa.'

'A total stranger,' Magnus added acerbically, surveying Craig without enthusiasm.

'Pa,' she said loudly, 'this is Robb's brother, Craig. We travelled together from Toronto.'

Her father's eyes were full of contempt and the anger she always seemed to evoke in him. 'By the way you look, it is more than travelling you have done——'

'That's enough!' Craig said sharply. 'I took the liberty of arriving early in the day to see if Marya would go to Viðoy with me for a picnic...the way she's dressed is nothing to do with me; she had no idea I was coming.'

Magnus drew himself to his full height. 'Here on the islands we are brought up to speak respectfully to our elders,' he thundered.

Marya winced. Craig said impassively, 'That's a good rule—as long as the elders also speak with respect to those who have done nothing to deserve otherwise.'

'She is wild, my daughter. Always she has been wild, no matter what I do. I speak to her how I choose!'

Craig said in a level voice, 'She is an honest and beautiful woman who has paid, I'm beginning to realise, in hard coin for a single mistake. You could do worse than choose to forgive her for that mistake, Mr Hansen.'

Magnus pushed his wool cap further askew with a gnarled hand. 'I do not come into my own house to be insulted,' he roared. 'Out!'

Craig said calmly, 'I'm going to wait here for Marya. Once she's ready, we'll both leave.' He crossed his arms over his chest, his big body perfectly relaxed, and smiled at Magnus.

Magnus was not used to being thwarted. His cheeks as red as the combs on a bantam rooster, he sputtered, 'You foreigners! I like to know what is wrong with a good man from Tjørnuvík——'

He was launched into a tirade Marya had heard many times before. She said clearly, 'Craig, I'll be ready in five minutes,' and ran for the stairs. And it was not until she reached the top that she realised that somehow she had agreed to spend the day with Craig.

So much for her grand resolutions, she thought, reaching into her wardrobe.

She put on beige trousers and a sweater she had knitted before she met Tony; the dark brown wool and intricate off-white pattern were traditionally Faroese. Two minutes dealt with her make-up. Then, after a brief hesitation, she brushed her hair smooth and fastened it at her nape with a brown velvet ribbon before hurrying downstairs.

Craig was standing patiently in the kitchen, and Magnus, perhaps because speaking English had slowed him down, was still on the rampage. He glared at his daughter. 'I should not allow you outside this door.'

Suddenly she had had enough. Not bothering to mask her pain, Marya said jaggedly, 'It's all right for Kathrin to go out with Robb, but not for me to go out with his brother—you always loved her better than me, Pa. Always!' She ran past him, hauled the door open and stumbled down the steps.

Craig's white car was parked near the door. She got in the passenger side, slammed the door and sat hunched in the seat. Craig got in beside her, started the engine and backed out of the narrow space between the houses, all without saying a word; not until he had traversed the curve of beach and climbed the cliff road far enough that Tjørnuvík was out of sight did he cross the road into a lay-by and turn off the engine. 'He does love you, Marya,' he said, just as if there had been no gap in the conversation. 'He doesn't rant and roar like that from indifference.'

'He hates me,' she muttered.

'That's the other face of love...do you have any idea why he would hate you?'

She shook her head. 'I wish I did know.'

'What happened to your mother? Is she dead?'

'She died when I was five—I hardly remember her.'

'Did she look like you?'

Marya glanced at him in surprise. 'I don't know...we don't have any pictures of her.'

'Did she have red hair, for instance?'

Marya said slowly, 'I have this image of me as a little girl sitting in my mother's lap on a rock wall in the sun...and her hair shining red as the feathers on our hens.' She stared down at her hands; she had not thought of that image for months.

'Maybe it's something to do with your mother—that you remind him of her in some way.'

In sudden excitement she said, 'Grethe might know.'

'Ask her,' said Craig.

Marya raised her head. His face was serious, the grey eyes gentle; he did not look at all like the hard-featured men who had frequented La Roulade. Nor did he look like Tony. He looked, she thought painfully, as a friend might look, a concerned and—it was the only word that came to mind—loving friend. She said, the words feeling awkward on her tongue, 'You defended me to my father... and you didn't let him turn you out of the house.'

'I didn't like the way he was speaking to you.'

She shivered. 'Maybe he saw us kissing each other.'

'What if he did? You're twenty-two, Marya—not fourteen.'

'Sometimes he makes me feel as if I'm fourteen,' she confessed.

'You made a mistake three years ago, and you've paid for it,' Craig said strongly. 'Put it behind you, Marya—and don't let people like your father make you pay for it forever.'

In her own way Kathrin had said the same thing. 'We'd better go,' Marya said, her eyes unfathomable. 'We're supposed to be finding Kathrin and Robb.'

'Think about what I said, won't you?'

He sounded grim, the gentleness gone from his face, and she was suddenly glad; the other Craig was much harder to deal with, for he did not fit her image of a rich man. She knew where she was with this one.

They started off again, the road following the coast to the bridge that spanned the channel between the islands of Stremoy and Eysturoy. The sun shone in an almost cloudless sky, the gulls like white flecks drifting on the warm air; the water was blue and calm, dotted with circular salmon weirs. And everywhere were the ridged, grass-covered hills where sheep roamed at will, and ice-cold water gurgled between the rocks, and wild flowers bloomed.

There were two tunnels through the mountains on Eysturoy, each well over a mile in length. Marya, who had been sitting in silence, preoccupied with thoughts that were far from pleasant, had forgotten about the tunnels; they always made her feel claustrophobic. And the ones on the next island were worse, for they were single-laned and unlit, and she had had two of the worst arguments in her life in the one that emerged on Hvanna Sound. One argument with her father, she thought wryly, and the other with Tony. How very appropriate.

In her present mood these memories seemed like the final straw. In the thick darkness of Eysturoy's second tunnel, she said caustically, 'You know, Craig, you're not behaving very logically.'

'Oh?' He did not sound encouraging.

'According to you, Kathrin's a gold-digger who'll do anything to get her hands on Robb's money. I'm Kathrin's sister, and I've already chased one rich man across the Atlantic. Yet here you are inviting me to form a partnership with you. Aren't you worried that I'm after your money, too?'

'Marya, you've done nothing but discourage me since the day we met.'

'But I didn't know you were rich until a couple of days ago. So I had no reason to encourage you.'

'You did your level best to slam the door in my face this morning.'

'Perhaps I was playing hard to get,' she said limpidly. 'As an antidote to all those other women who were un-subtle enough to chase you. After all, look what happened next. I wasn't exactly fighting you off then, was I?'

The car burst out into the sunlight. Craig said shortly, 'Stop it, Marya.'

'Think about it, Craig...I've just spent all my savings to get here, and I've quit both my jobs. A million dollars—that was the amount you mentioned, I believe—could be quite an incentive, couldn't it?'

Tight-lipped, Craig drove down the slope towards the wharf where they would catch the ferry to the island of Borðoy. 'You're different,' he grated. 'I know you are.'

But she had planted the seeds of doubt, Marya knew. And knew, too, why she had behaved so meanly. She did not want to fall in love again; and the danger in Craig lay not so much in his sexual attraction, powerful though that was, as in his kindness, the rare, disarming gentleness that added to his masculinity rather than detracting from it.

So she would make sure he would not feel kindly towards her.

Her conscience told her she was being horribly manipulative; her reason told her she was merely protecting herself. As Craig parked in the queue she said brightly, 'It'll be fifteen minutes until we board...I'm going for a walk.'

'I'll stay with the car,' he said grimly.

She walked back up the road and clambered down a grassy slope to the water. Orange lichen encrusted the rocks, in whose crevices blossomed the small pink spheres of seathrift. The brassy yellow of marsh marigolds edged a little stream that trickled down to the sea. It was very quiet.

The words came into her mind as clearly as if they were written there. We could make love here, Craig and I.

Then the whistle blared on the ferry and Marya scrambled up the bank as if a dozen men were after her, and ran back to the car, reaching it just as Craig was about to drive on board. He said without noticeable emotion, 'I thought you'd decided to stay behind. Or would that be playing a bit too hard to get?'

She gave him what she hoped was a mysterious smile and said, 'I think it would.'

'I don't know what to make of you, Marya Hansen— do you know that?'

She looked at him through her lashes. 'That must make a change for you.'

He eased the car into the allotted space and hauled on the handbrake. 'Maybe I should have thought twice about this so-called partnership.'

'With a million dollars I could take a Ph.D. in biology,' Marya said dreamily, getting out of the car.

'Don't think small, Marya—why not buy up the whole department?' he replied with a wolfish grin.

She did not trust that grin. Moreover, as she closed the car door she noticed a picnic basket on the back seat; so Craig had taken it for granted that she would spend the day with him. Finding she disliked this assumption quite a lot, she followed the other passengers to the upper deck and stationed herself near the bow; watching absorbedly as the ferry left the village of Leirvík and headed towards the channel between Kalsoy and Borðoy. Craig had followed and was standing beside her. He said conversationally, although his eyes were watchful on her face, 'Did I mention to you that I'm thinking of buying Kathrin off?'

If he had wanted a reaction, he was soon satisfied. Marya looked at him in utter disbelief. 'You mean, offer her money to leave Robb alone?'

'That's the general idea ... how much do you think it would take?'

'More than you've got,' she said rudely. 'That's just the sort of thing someone like you would think of. Money can buy everything—that's the way you operate, isn't it? You and all your kind. Oh, you're intolerable!'

'So it wouldn't buy you, Marya?'

'No!'

He said silkily, 'That's not what you were saying in the tunnel.'

He had set the trap and she had walked right into it. Furious with herself, she tried to recoup the ground she had lost. With all the haughtiness at her command she said, 'That doesn't necessarily mean I'm not interested in your money.'

'Now who's being illogical?' Then his gaze sharpened. 'What's that over there?'

She turned to see, felt his fingers whip the ribbon away from her hair and heard him say, 'There—that's better.'

'That was a very childish trick!'

'Laugh, Marya,' Craig said kindly. 'The world's always better for a bit of laughter.'

The breeze that was stirring the curls on her shoulders was also playing with his hair, and his eyes were dancing. The smooth, tanned muscles of his forearms, the tangle of body hair at his throat, the flat belly under his shirt: she was aware of them all, and wondered if she would ever forget him, this tall stranger whose purpose was the same as hers yet who was so much at odds with her.

He said in a low voice, 'When you look at me like that, all I want to do is kiss you.'

With desperate truth Marya said, 'Craig, I wish I'd never met you.'

Abruptly she turned away from him, staring into the channel where the tidal currents churned under the surface. She couldn't fall in love again. She mustn't. She'd be making the same mistake twice in a row...she'd be an utter fool.

CHAPTER SIX

THE ferry docked in the busy harbour of Klaksvík, where draggers bedecked with pink marker buoys were moored along the wharves and screaming flocks of gulls clustered around the fish plant. The two single-laned tunnels that had been cut through the mountains of Borðoy had only ten seconds of daylight between one and the next; Marya suffered through them in silence, knowing the return trip would be worse because they would not have the right of way. Craig then drove across the short causeway to Viðoy and travelled north until they came to the scattered houses of Vidareiði at the head of the bay.

'I don't see Robb's car,' he muttered, gazing down at the village.

'The road cuts across to the other shore—perhaps they've gone there.'

But although they followed the road until it became nothing but a dirt track too rough for a car, there was no sign of Robb and Kathrin. Craig turned off the ignition, his mouth set. Marya got out of the car, stretching her legs. She was deeply relieved; she did not want more conflict, another fight with her sister. Anyway, she thought unhappily, how could she blame Kathrin for wanting to be with Robb when she herself wanted to fall into Craig's arms every time he looked at her?

'They're not here,' Craig said tightly, stating the obvious. 'Do you think we could have missed them in ~ík?'

'We might have, I suppose. Although if Kathrin's as intent on getting pregnant as you seem to think she is, this is a more likely spot than the fish plant in Klaksvík.' Marya gave him a baleful look. 'How did you know they were coming here?'

'Robb told the receptionist when he ordered their picnic.'

A little devil made her say, 'Maybe he's fooled you. Maybe they went west instead of east—to Vágar. The airport's in Vágar.' She gazed soulfully up at the sky. 'And it's a beautiful sunny day for flying.'

Craig grabbed her by the arm. He was patently un-amused by her suggestion; in fact, he looked murder-ous. 'Do you know something I don't?'

Marya put her nose in the air as if the fish plant were right beside her. 'I have no idea where Kathrin is.'

His grip tightened. 'Would you tell me if you did?'

'I might not,' she answered recklessly. 'Because I'm glad we didn't find them—we're acting like a morality squad! Hoping to catch them making love on the hillside...judging by the way we were carrying on in the kitchen this morning, we're not exactly in a position to cast the first stone.'

'Are you saying you *want* them to get married?'

'I'd like to know why you automatically assume that my sister's after your brother's money,' she flared. 'You called me a man-hater—I think you're a woman-hater.'

Her anger ignited his own. '*You* try growing up with a very rich man for a father. The word gets around, be-lieve me—you're labelled. People look at you and see dollar signs, not a real person, and they make friends with you for what you can do for them, not because they like you. And then you start dating, and the mothers push their daughters at you, and the pretty girls all flirt with you and expect to be taken to places like La

Roulade—as long as you pick up the tab—and pretty soon you know damn well that you're being taken.' Craig broke off, raking his fingers through his hair. 'Hell, what's the use? Because I know what you're going to say—it's easy to complain when you've got the money. And, of course, you're right. But don't ever think that it doesn't alter the way people see you!'

Marya stared at him in silence; she was taken aback, for it was a novel viewpoint, not one she had considered before, and she needed time to assimilate it. Craig gave her arm another shake; although he still looked formidably angry, she had the idea he was already regretting his outburst. 'Did they go to Vágar, Marya?'

'I don't know! I'm only glad they're not here.'

'You don't back down, do you?' he snarled. 'I'll say that for you.'

It was an ungenerous compliment, but a compliment nevertheless. 'Craig,' Marya said energetically, 'fighting makes me hungry, we've got a picnic in the car, and it's a sunny day. Sunny days are not so frequent in the Faroes that one can afford to ignore them. So why don't we forget about my sister and your brother for half an hour? A lunch break. Then we can always go back to fighting again—we can fight all the way to Vágar if that's what you want to do.'

His fingers loosened their hold and he gave her a crooked smile, matching her change of mood. 'Sure,' he said. 'Good idea. But first I think we should kiss and make up.'

She pulled away, torn between laughter and panic. 'I don't think that's necessary.'

'Only one kiss—I promise.'

Swiftly, before she could protest further, he took her in his arms and found her mouth with his, and as the sun shone on her closed lids Marya discovered that one kiss could be a very comprehensive experience. She was out of breath when Craig freed her, her breast rising and falling, her knees feeling quite unreliable. He said, a glint in his eye, 'That's more fun than fighting.'

She was in total agreement. 'Get the picnic, Craig,' she croaked.

He spread a couple of jackets on the grass and unpacked the basket, and they munched on chicken and egg sandwiches and drank lemonade. In front of them the sea sparkled in the sun, the low peak of Svínoy and the gaunt cliffs of Fugloy on the horizon; sheep bleated on the hillside behind them, and a black and white ewe wandered over to investigate them, her coat matted in long, dirty strands that hung to the ground, her black nose testing the air.

Forgetting that Craig was a rich man whom she hated, Marya chattered on about the summer shearing and the autumn round-up, and how she and Grethe used to card and spin the wool to be knitted into sweaters like the one she was wearing. She then ate a piece of nut cake and finished off with an apple; she felt very happy.

Craig had stretched out on the grass beside her, his eyes shut, his shirt taut across his chest. Marya threw the apple core at the sheep, which caused it to skitter away in alarm; and decided that it was in her own best interests to skitter away from Craig. The only alternative seemed to be to attack him, she thought with wry honesty, getting to her feet and crossing the dirt track to the field that stretched to the edge of the cliff. Had she felt this way with Tony? She was sure she had not.

Her brow creased in thought, she wandered down the slope, stooping to pick a bunch of sweetly scented thyme. She had loved Tony, but she had not been shaken to the core by desire, the way she was with Craig. Yet she did not love Craig. She hated all he stood for... didn't she?

The tiny pink flowers gave her no answers. She added buttercups and clover to her bouquet, watched the sheep grazing at the very brink of the cliff, and wondered if, given the choice, she would rather be back at La Roulade in her safe, controlled little world of a week ago, or here on Vidoy with a man who both fascinated and frightened her.

'Marya! We'd better go.'

She turned. Craig was waving to her from the track. Taking her time, she walked up the hill.

'Come on,' he said impatiently. 'We should get back— I didn't mean to fall asleep.'

She found herself strongly reluctant to leave, for going back meant facing Kathrin and Magnus. 'What's the hurry?'

'I guess I want to find out if they have gone to Vágar— the more I think about it, the more likely it is.'

'If they have, you're too late to stop them. And if they haven't, you don't have to worry,' she said flippantly.

He was loading the basket and jackets in the back seat of the car, and something in the set of his shoulders caused her to add, with a sense of foreboding, 'If they haven't, you're not still thinking of trying to buy Kathrin off?'

He straightened. 'Yeah...I was thinking I might try that,' he said.

Being with him was like being at the mercy of the tides, Marya thought fancifully. High tide, low tide. Attract, repel. Kind, then ruthless. And she, washed back and forth, at the mercy of currrents beyond her control.

In silence she got in the car and fastened her seatbelt. They bounced along the track and joined the road again, passing the brightly coloured houses and the squat little church of Vidareidi. Across the sound at the foot of the high peaks of Bordoy nestled the tiny settlement of Múli that could be reached only by boat; as the sun danced on the water, she saw, on the other side of the causeway at the base of the mountain, the small round entrance to the first tunnel. She said stiffly, 'Travelling this way in the tunnel, you have to pull off for oncoming traffic.'

'I thought it was too easy coming over,' he said drily. 'Quite a feat of engineering, isn't it?'

Marya was bracing herself for the plunge into darkness, and did not reply. Craig looked as though he were enjoying himself. Whistling under his breath, he drove across the causeway and into the tunnel.

The darkness was absolute, more brown than black, so opaque that their headlights were too feeble to pierce it for more than a few feet. The curving walls and roof of the tunnel had been gouged out of bare rock, from which water dripped, collecting in murky puddles on the dirt road. Gearing down, Craig said jauntily, 'How do you know where the pull-offs are?'

'You don't—you just hope you reach one before the oncoming traffic reaches you. If not, you back up.'

He gave what she considered an entirely inappropriate snort of laughter. Then, peering through the windscreen, he said, 'Aren't those headlights?'

Two small yellow circles had appeared, although the darkness was such that it was impossible to tell how far away they were. 'The first pull-off should be on our right,' Marya said tensely.

'Relax, Marya....either we make it or we back out.'

How could she relax when dirty water was splashing on the windscreen and the whole weight of the mountain was overhead? She scrunched lower in her seat; the headlights were approaching with alarming speed.

'We can pull off just ahead,' said Craig. He was still whistling.

The pull-offs were nothing but hollows blasted in the rock face, boulders still lying in tumbled heaps on the ground, which was awash with water. The car lurched as close to the wall as Craig could get. He put it in neutral and rolled down his window.

The air stank of exhaust fumes and stagnant water, and to Marya's mind of something else far more threatening: something as ancient as the rocks themselves, that would outlast every living soul on the islands. Because sound was trapped, the noise of the two cars echoed and re-echoed, bouncing off the rock with a hollow throbbing as loud as a train. Like the heartbeat of the mountain, she thought, and said tautly, 'Close the window!'

Craig looked over at her. 'Hey,' he said, 'there's nothing to be scared of.' Then he reached over to put an arm around her.

Tony had put his arm around her in just the same way. She struck Craig's hand away. 'Don't!'

There had been repugnance in her voice. Craig said nastily, 'Have you forgotten the million dollars, Marya?'

Under the circumstances it was the worst possible thing he could have said. He *was* like Tony, she thought sickly. Sooner or later everything had its price.

As the other car passed them, the momentary brightness of its headlights shone in her distraught face and wild eyes. Biting off the words, she said, 'I wouldn't touch you for five million dollars!'

The blackness swallowed them again. Craig eased out of the pull-off and said, 'You'd do anything for five million dollars, Marya.'

'I would not! You seem to think—what's that?'

There was a flashing gold light somewhere ahead of them. 'Let's go find out,' Craig said, and forged into the tunnel again.

Marya huddled into her corner in utter wretchedness. Craig did not trust her any more than she trusted him. He, at some deep level, could not believe she was indifferent to his money; she, at the slightest chance, reverted to all her prejudices about rich men. She discovered she was shivering, and with all her heart longed to be out in the sunshine again.

The flashing gold light was on top of a big truck parked in the middle of the road right beside a pull-off. Craig tucked his car out of the way and murmured, 'A repair truck of some kind.'

Halfway through the mountain Marya did not want to consider what might need repairing. She closed her eyes, found the darkness, and opened them again. Craig said irritably, 'Why didn't you tell me you were terrified of tunnels?'

Tony had asked much the same question. 'It's only this one,' she mumbled.

One of the repairmen was standing in the road chatting to the driver; praying that they would move, focusing all her will-power on them in a frantic bid to get out of the tunnel, she did not notice Craig hesitate, then, with the air of a man making a decision, reach out to pull her into his arms. The shock of his touch ran through her body; she struck out blindly at his chest with her fists and burst into tears.

The tears, once started, would not stop. She cried for the innocent nineteen-year-old whom Tony had betrayed, for the crushing loneliness of her first winter in Toronto, for the ugly boarding houses she had lived in and the mean little restaurants where she had worked. She cried for her father, who did not love her, and for her sister, who was angry with her. And she cried for finding comfort and security in the arms of a man she did not trust.

A sharp, repetitive tapping penetrated her distress. As she pushed Craig away and fumbled for her shoulder-bag in the dark, she heard him roll the window down and one of the workmen say in Faroese, 'Is she ill? Do you need help?'

Craig, of course, did not understand a word. Marya stammered with at least partial truth, 'I'm all right—I get claustrophobic in tunnels.'

'Ah . . . we'll move the truck so you can get through.' With a flourish worthy of a knight of old he bowed from the waist, then waved the truck forward.

Marya blew her nose. Craig signalled his thanks and pulled out on the road again. The car bounced through the puddles, the headlights glancing off the rock walls. They met one more vehicle, and she suffered through the wait in silence, still trying to get her breathing under control; she had not totally succeeded in doing so when the car emerged into the light.

The second tunnel was only a few feet away, its entrance at an angle to the first one. Craig pulled over on the narrow shoulder of the road, put on the handbrake and said flatly, 'You haven't cried like that for years. Not once when you were in Toronto, I'd be willing to bet.'

Marya let out her breath in a long sigh; she felt very tired, certainly too tired for anything but the truth. 'At first I didn't dare,' she said, gazing down at the twisted handkerchief in her lap. 'I was afraid if I started I'd never be able to stop. Then after a while it was as if there was a kind of armour around me that separated my emotions from the world outside . . . so I couldn't cry, not even if I'd wanted to.'

'I see.' He said, even more grimly, 'Why did you strike out at me when I tried to take you into my arms?'

'Because of Tony,' she said with forlorn accuracy.

'You thought I was *Tony*?'

She looked up, and instinctively laid one hand on his forearm. 'No! But the only time Tony and I ever went through that tunnel, he got angry with me. It brought it all back—that's what I meant.'

'Why was he angry?' Craig demanded.

'Now you're angry, too,' she wailed.

'For God's sake, Marya, I'm not angry with you!'

Not totally convinced, she muttered, 'It was dark and there weren't any other cars and he thought it would be fun if we...fooled around a bit. When I told him I hated the tunnel, he didn't believe me. He thought,' she gulped, 'I was just playing hard to get.'

'Nice guy.'

Craig's sarcasm made her wince. 'I see now that I should have paid more attention to the way he behaved. But I was too young and naïve to know anything about men, and I had no one to ask. I couldn't talk to my father. Kathrin was too young to ask about sex, and Grethe too nice. Besides, right after that Tony said we'd get married.'

'Is he still in Toronto?'

A smile wavered on her lips. 'He came into the restaurant once. With a woman. I put on my most supercilious hostess manner, and he never came back.'

'Good for you.' Then Craig's voice changed. 'Do you know something, Marya? This is the first time you've ever touched me.'

She suddenly became aware that her hand was still resting on his arm, and became aware, too, of the warmth of his skin, the roughness of hair and the latent strength of the smoothly bunched muscles. She snatched her hand away and cried, 'We don't even *like* each other!'

'Don't we? Or is it that we've never allowed ourselves to see each other as real people?'

The grey eyes held her pinioned. 'What do you mean?' she faltered.

'I've had far too many women chase me for my money—so I look at a woman and I see dollar signs in her eyes. You've seen rather too much of how rich men behave, so you look at me and your brain says, look out, he's a rich man, don't trust him. When are we going to get beyond those stereotypes, Marya? To find the real you and the real me.'

With a visible effort Marya looked away. 'I...don't even know if I want to,' she said, and had no idea if she was speaking the truth or an outright lie.

'Give it some thought,' he rasped.

Her head jerked up at the tone of his voice. He was reaching for the gear shift, checking the rearview mirror; his profile looked as if it were carved in stone, and the line of his shoulders was full of tension.

She had hurt him; this issue of reality must be very important to him. She had the sudden mad impulse to throw her arms around him and hold him as tightly as she could because she did not care one whit for his money. But he had pulled out on the road again and the darkness of the second tunnel had quickly swallowed them, and her impulse died stillborn.

This tunnel had lights, and the pull-offs were marked with square blue signs; within a few minutes they were driving down the coast to Klaksvík. A ferry was loading at the dock, so they drove straight on. But as Marya got out of the car and headed for the metal steps to the upper deck, she came face to face with a young woman with a mop of blonde curls who was also heading for the steps. Kathrin. Robb was at her heels.

Kathrin gaped at her sister. 'You've been crying,' she said, and turned on Craig like a virago. 'What have you been doing to her?'

Touched that her sister had flown so instinctively to her defence, Marya exclaimed, 'It wasn't his fault! It was the tunnel.'

'The one on Bordoy? That's right—you had a fight with Pa in that tunnel, didn't you? And you always did hate it.'

'I didn't hear about that fight,' said Craig.

Marya said hastily, 'It was four years ago—I'd asked Pa if he'd help pay for me to go to university in Copenhagen. But he wouldn't. He said Tjørnuvík was good enough for him, so it should be good enough for me.' She grimaced. 'One more reason why I ran away with Tony.'

Kathrin said suspiciously, 'What were you doing on Viðoy, anyway? It must have been something pretty important for you to brave that tunnel.'

Marya looked the picture of guilt. Craig said blandly, 'We were following you.'

As Kathrin began to sputter in fury, Robb took her by the elbow and said with unmistakable authority, 'What else would you expect, Kathrin? Come on, we're going up on deck.' He gave Marya a non-committal nod and half pushed, half steered Kathrin up the stairs.

Fighting down the urge to run after them, Marya waited until they were out of earshot and said shrewishly, 'You forgot to try and buy her off.'

'So I did.'

The deck vibrated and the wake hissed as the ferry left the dock. In exasperation Marya said, 'I'll tell you something else, Craig Huntingdon—I don't think your brother's at all the impressionable young fool you seem to think he is. He certainly knows how to handle Kathrin.'

'Yeah...I can see a lot of changes in him,' Craig acknowledged slowly, running his fingers through his hair.

'He was a playboy a year ago, a fun-loving kid without a thought in his head beyond the next ski trip. Then he did what I did at his age. Took off around the world on his own with a very limited budget—that's how he ended up in the Faroes. He's grown up since then, I can really see the difference...'

'But he still doesn't know a gold-digger when he meets one,' she retorted.

'Stereotypes, Marya?' Craig said, raising one brow.

'We're supposed to be up on deck,' she said crossly, and flounced up the steps.

Kathrin and Robb were at the bow; she marched to the stern and stared at a pair of guillemots on the water as if they were the most fascinating sight in the world. She was the one in danger of becoming a virago, she thought with rather desperate humour. Maybe it was all those months of being the perfect hostess. Or maybe it was nothing to do with La Roulade. Maybe she could blame it instead on her emotional instability whenever Craig Huntingdon came within ten feet of her.

The land of maybe... it would be nice for once to be sure of just one thing.

Craig dropped Marya off at her father's house late in the afternoon. He did not suggest another meeting. Grethe had baked a haddock for dinner, Marya cleaned up the kitchen afterwards, and then, too restless to sit still, went for a walk. When she came back across the bridge to the village, Mrs Rasmussen's lace curtain twitched, a signal that Marya was being watched. Mrs Rasmussen was the village gossip, who owned one of the few telephones in the village. Not stopping to think, Marya ran up her steps and knocked on the door.

Mrs Rasmussen's house was a minefield of fussy little pieces of furniture and hooked rugs that skidded on the wooden floors; but her brass ornaments twinkled and shone, for she polished them as she kept watch at the window, and her four well-fed cats fawned around Marya's ankles. Mrs Rasmussen had outlived three husbands, and first Marya had to listen to all the details of the demise of Emil, the most recent one. Then she was peppered with questions, which she answered with a mixture of candour and wariness, about her years in Canada and the fate of the handsome young man with the black hair. Finally it was Marya's turn. 'Mrs Rasmussen,' she said, 'can you tell me anything about my mother? Did she look like me, for instance?'

Mrs Rasmussen poured two more cups of ink-black coffee and settled back in her chair, her gentian-blue eyes gleaming: an invitation to gossip was as good as a new husband. 'Indeed she did. I never thought she'd end up with someone like your father. A good man, Magnus,' she added quickly. 'But strict. Your mother loved to roam the fields and talk to the sheep and the birds... wild, she was. But she settled down a bit when you were born—as women have to.'

Marya stroked the fat tabby cat that had plunked itself in her lap. 'Did she love my father? And did he love her?'

'She must have... she married him, and she was not one to do so for convenience or security. As for him, he loved her, yes—too much, maybe. Because I don't think he ever understood her, or quite trusted that she would stay with him. She was like the sea wind—you can't trap it inside the four walls of a house.' Mrs Rasmussen took a sip of coffee and said delicately, 'There was talk she might have been unfaithful to him. But I myself doubt that. Had she fallen in love with someone else she would have moved out of your father's house and into the new man's...because that's the way she was. She stayed with your father until the day she died.'

Mrs Rasmussen gave a satisfied sigh, for it was a gratifyingly sad ending to a romantic story. 'In child-birth,' she added. 'A stillborn son.'

Marya already knew this. She asked bluntly, 'Who was she supposed to have had an affair with?'

'A man from Saksun—Petur Neilsen. So they said.'

'They' had undoubtedly included Mrs Rasmussen. Marya quelled a flicker of anger, for she had been given an image of her mother that she could both relate to and cherish; there had been the same wildness in herself for as long as she could remember. Politely she finished her coffee and gave out a discreet amount of infor-mation on Kathrin's young man; then she got up to go. From Mrs Rasmussen's fussy little house she went straight to the boat-shed, before she could lose her nerve.

But Magnus was not there; he must be playing cards with some of his old cronies. Frustrated, she went back to the house, pushed the door open, and heard someone moving about upstairs. 'Kathrin? Is that you?'

Her sister's voice wafted down the stairs, as imper-sonal as a stranger's. 'I'm getting some clothes.'

Marya trailed up the stairs to the bedroom under the eaves, where Kathrin had thrown part of the contents of her wardrobe on her bed, her skirts and blouses a bouquet of bright colours. 'I wish you'd stay here tonight, not at Grethe's,' Marya said impulsively. 'I feel terrible that we're so at odds. I promise I won't even mention Robb's name.'

Kathrin held up a brief flowered skirt, then tossed it aside. 'It doesn't matter if you do. In a way you and Craig have been good for us—you've shown us how much we really do love each other.' She hung a couple of blouses back in the wardrobe and said, her eyes on

her sister, 'We're going to get married in September. Here
in the village, or else in the old church at Kirkjubøur.'

For a moment all the prejudices of the last three years
hovered on Marya's tongue: he's a rich man, you can't
trust him, he'll abandon you and break your heart. She
took a deep breath and said steadily, 'I hope you'll both
be very happy, Kathrin.'

Kathrin's smile was generous; she was not one to hold
a grudge. 'We will be, I know.'

Ruefully Marya said, 'All of a sudden I feel like the
younger sister, as if you know more than I do.' She took
another long breath; this seemed to be her day for asking
questions. 'Kathrin,' she said awkwardly, 'what's it
like—no, I can't ask that. What I mean is, I didn't really
like——'

'Making love, you mean?' Kathrin finished kindly.
'It's wonderful, Marya. The most wonderful feeling in
the world.'

Kathrin was smiling a small, secret smile. Marya felt
a pang of envy. 'It wasn't like that for me and Tony,'
she blurted.

'Then he wasn't the right man,' Kathrin said with all
the authority of one who was very much in love. 'Don't
ever settle for less.'

Good advice, Marya supposed. But what did it mean?

CHAPTER SEVEN

KATHRIN had gone to work when Marya woke up the next morning; they had talked far into the night, catching up on the years that Marya had been away, and had only stopped when Magnus banged on the ceiling with his stick. The little bedroom was already warm, and when Marya peered through the tiny panes of glass she saw another clear and sunny day. She dressed in a full cotton skirt and an embroidered white blouse that laced across her breasts, with old leather thongs on her feet, and ran downstairs, singing to herself. She had accomplished a lot yesterday, she thought as she filled the kettle. She had made peace with her sister, and she had found the information she needed to make peace with her father.

She paused at the window, where the Giant and the Witch stood guard over the bay, and sea and sky met in a knife-sharp edge. The tunnel through the mountain on Borðoy had finally done her a favour, she thought soberly. She had needed that storm of weeping, for she had held back her tears for far too long.

Her hands stilled on the handle of the kettle as an image of Craig dropped into her mind. Craig, it seemed, was going to be her brother-in-law. Tied to her for life. Would she ever make peace with him?

She cut a chunk of bread off one of Grethe's home-made loaves and chewed on it thoughtfully. When the tea was made, she filled two mugs, and carried them down the steps and over to the boat-house. Magnus was sanding one of the square Faroese oars. She passed him his mug, perched on a stool and said, 'Good morning, Pa.'

He grunted a reply. She took a sip of tea, cupped her hands around the steaming mug, and plunged right in. 'Pa, there's something I really need to know, so please don't mind me asking...do I remind you of Mama?' The childish name had come to her tongue without thought; and an any more subtle approach would have been wasted on Magnus.

His hand stilled. 'What kind of a question is that?'

'It's a question I want the answer to, Pa—because it's important.' The words tripped from her tongue. 'I think the reason you've always favoured Kathrin is because she doesn't remind you of anyone except herself, whereas every time you look at me you see my mother, not me. She had red hair, didn't she? And maybe we even act the same way—you always said I was wild and——'

'*Stop!*'

Some of Marya's tea slopped on her lap. She sat still and knew with a burgeoning of fear and excitement that she had come very close to the truth, for Magnus's cheeks were mottled an angry red. But his eyes were the cold blue of the winter ice in the bay, and when he spoke his voice sent shivers up her spine.

'Your mother is dead...dead these many years. There will be no more talk of her—do you hear me?'

Marya clutched the mug so hard her fingers hurt. 'She was my mother!' she cried. 'You can't act as if she didn't exist.'

'I act as I please in my own house, my own boat-shed.' He gestured so violently with the oar that she leaned backwards on the stool. 'You will not talk of her again, Marya.'

The wildness that had caused Marya to roam the hills and take her father's boat out on the bay when he had expressly forbidden her to do so shone in her eyes, changing them from grey to green. But she tamped down her instinctive, angry response. Putting her mug on an upended box, she leaned forward. 'Pa, I think you loved Mama very much. So of course it would be painful for you if I reminded you of her, and you might easily resent me . . . just tell me that that's the way it was—so I'll understand.' So I can forgive you, she added inwardly.

His voice was like the hissing of the ice shards that rose and fell on the winter swells. 'I will not listen to more of this talk.'

And because she was frightened, Marya's anger overcame caution and restraint. 'I'm not fifteen any more . . . I'm twenty-two, and I have a right to the truth. You thought she was unfaithful to you, didn't you? So you've been angry with her ever since, and angry with me because I remind you of her. You don't really hate me—you hate your memories of her!'

Magnus got to his feet, brandishing the oar. It hit the mug of tea she had brought him, which inscribed an arc through the air, crashed to the floor and smashed into pieces. Wood shavings swirled in the puddle of spilled tea. 'Get out of here!' he roared.

Marya scrambled off the stool and ran for the door. She banged it shut behind her, an action that made her feel minimally better, and hurried between the houses to the track that led to the wharf, praying she would not meet anyone she knew. She had no clear destination in mind, only to be closer to the sea, that had always been a source of comfort for her. Her red skirt a bright patch of colour, her hands thrust in her pockets, she marched along the path, head downbent, and all her emotions marched with her.

But under an untidy mélange of anger and pain rested a small, clear thought: Magnus could not bear to talk about his long-dead wife. And what better reason than the one Mrs Rasmussen had put forward, that he had suspected his wife of infidelity? Her steps slowing, she realised he had not looked surprised when she, Marya, had suggested this. He had merely been outraged, and had got rid of her as fast as he could.

She stopped altogether, listening to the water trickle down the side of the hill, where buttercups and red campion were tangled in the grass. So what was she to do now?

Her shoulders slumped. The gravel crunching under her sandals, she walked past the empty sheep pens to the wharf. The concrete had been poured in the middle of living rock; two rowing boats were moored alongside, and with a surge of remembrance she recognised the smaller of the two as the one Magnus had built six years ago at Kathrin's request. The stem was carved into a stylised dragon's head and the name of the boat was inscribed on a plaque near the bow. *Kathrin*, the boat was called. Not Marya.

'Marya!'

With a start she looked around, almost expecting to see a red-haired woman hailing her from the path, only in delayed reaction realising it had been a man's voice.

The man was Craig. After Magnus, she thought wildly, he was the last man she wanted to see. She bent to untie the hawser, and out of the corner of her eye saw him begin to run along the wharf.

Her fingers had lost none of their nimbleness. She tossed the rope into the boat, clasping the gunwales as she climbed in, hampered by her full skirt. Then she reached for one of the oars to push off.

But Craig had reached her, and had grabbed the prow with one hand, holding the boat to the edge of the wharf. Her eyes glittering, Marya said, 'Let go, Craig.'

He was kneeling on the concrete, his cotton trousers pulled tight across his thighs, the muscles taut in his arm. 'Where are you going?'

'None of your business!'

'We've got beyond that stage, Marya. And you might as well tell me—because I won't let you go until you do.'

'Denmark?' she said in a voice like a whiplash. 'Norway?'

'Then you'll need a second oarsman,' he said, and quickly climbed in, sitting across from her on the other thwart.

'You're facing the wrong way,' she fumed. 'Craig, I don't want company, and what are you doing here anyway? I thought your main aim in life was to brandish fifty million dollars under my sister's nose.'

'She's working. I haven't got fifty million. Why are you in such a royal rage, my darling Marya?'

The tenderness in his eyes threw her totally off balance. 'Don't call me that!' she snapped. 'Go away and leave me alone.'

The boat was drifting away from the wharf on the clear, blue-green water, and from the hillside came the harsh call of an oystercatcher. His hands resting on his knees, his big body looking perfectly relaxed, Craig said, 'But I'd have to swim, and you wouldn't want me to perish of hypothermia right in front of your eyes, would you? Besides, you didn't answer my question.'

Her hands were gripping the oars, the smooth, varnished wood reminding her how Magnus had shaken the oar at her in anger. Craig was not going to go away, she thought. He was entirely capable of drifting on the bay for the rest of the day if that was what it took; and his calmness, the latent strength she was beginning, ephemerally, to trust, somehow encouraged her to speak. She looked him in the eye. 'I tried to make peace with my father this morning... but I didn't do very well.' Briefly she relayed what she had found out from Mrs Rasmussen, and her father's reaction. 'So that's that,' she finished hopelessly, and let one hand trail over the side in the cold water.

'Is this Petur—what was his name?'

'Petur Nielsen.'

'Is he still alive?'

'I don't know... he used to live in a little place called Saksun. There was a trail across the hills before the road was built, it would only have been three miles from Tjørnuvík.'

'We could go and see him. Ask him if your mother had an affair with him.'

'We can't do that!'

'Why not, Marya? It's a long time ago, and he'd have no reason to lie.'

She looked at him in consternation. 'You make everything seem so simple.'

Craig shrugged. 'It's obviously important to you. So if it's important, you do something about it.'

'I suppose so.' She gave him a sudden wide smile. 'We'll do it!'

He smiled back. 'We could go for a row first though, couldn't we? It's such a beautiful day—didn't you tell me days like this are rare in the Faroes?'

Marya hesitated, knowing exactly where she wanted to take him, wondering if it was wise. 'I could take you to my favourite place in the whole world,' she said slowly. 'If you want me to.'

Something unguarded showed in Craig's face; she saw that she had taken him by surprise. He answered with a formality that she found very touching, 'I would be honoured.'

'I never took Tony there,' she burst out, and could have bitten her tongue off.

He leaned forward, so close she could see the slate-grey of his irises. 'So why me, Marya?'

'I don't know,' she mumbled.

The tenderness was back in his face. 'Let's not worry about reasons and motives. It's a beautiful day, I'm with a beautiful woman, and I'd like the chance to use these rather peculiar oars. Why are they square?'

Grateful that he had given her something safe to discuss, for the look in his eyes had filled her with confusion shot through with a joy as buoyant as the sparkling sea, Marya explained, 'They're more safely seated than a normal oar, so the fishermen could row close to the cliffs and headlands when the tides were running. And the men had to row such long distances that feathering the oars would have damaged their wrists...Pa built this boat. Many's the time I've heard him repeat the old saying that a boatless man is a man in chains...'

Craig swivelled on the seat so his back was to her, and inserted a pair of the oars in the thole pins. 'It's two years since I've done any rowing,' he said cheerfully.

'It's three since I have,' she responded. 'Ready?'

Within five minutes they were rowing smoothly in unison, the water rippling against the sides of the boat and opening into a V-shaped wake. Marya tried to concentrate on anything but the play of muscles under Craig's shirt, and failed utterly; she was glad his back was to her.

They hugged the cliffs, the craggy volcanic rock streaked with bird droppings and patched with multi-coloured lichens; high overhead tufts of grass hung over the edge, and they saw a ram with long, curved horns scrambling from outcrop to outcrop. It bleated at them belligerently, then leaped out of sight. 'Don't they ever fall in?' Craig asked over his shoulder.

'The shepherds keep an eye out for them. But a few drown every year.'

The cliffs were getting steeper by the minute. The first cave appeared, a black hollow in the rock, the shallow water a gemlike turquoise. 'Your favourite place?' Craig quipped.

'Are you kidding? Too much like the tunnel...'

Because they had rounded the headland, the village was out of sight, and the two of them could have been alone in the world. The plash of the oars and the drip of water, the gentle gurgle of the swell and the warmth of the sun filled Marya with contentment. Magnus seemed a long way away, and Tony even further, for Tony would not have enjoyed this expedition at all. Craig was enjoying it, she thought. He was gazing up at the cliff, the sun gleaming like gold in his thick hair, his eyes intent. 'Aren't those nesting birds up there?' he asked.

Delighted with him for noticing, she said, 'Guillemots. And probably some razorbills...and look, there's a puffin.'

The puffin was skating across the surface of the water, wings pumping madly, bright feet flapping behind. As it veered its course, its brilliantly striped beak glinted in the light. 'If we don't make too much noise, we'll see more,' she said.

The guillemots were complaining in guttural chorus at this intrusion in their territory. Then the boat rounded an outcrop and Marya said, 'Look ahead of us, Craig.'

A huge needle of rock had been sheared from the face of the cliff, pointing skywards like an accusing finger. Fulmars skimmed through the gap as gracefully as

trapeze artists. Around its base puffins plopped under-
water and resurfaced in tiny explosions of spray.

As Marya rested on the oars, the boat wafted in a slow
circle. For several minutes she and Craig watched the
antics of the seabirds in silence, before he said quietly,
'A wonderful place...thank you for bringing me here,
Marya.'

He had turned in his seat and was smiling at her, a
smile without guile or hidden messages, and in a flash
of intuition she knew she felt closer to Craig now than
she ever had with Tony, even in the rose-strewn hotel
room, for Craig was in harmony with her world in a way
Tony had never been. She stammered, 'You're welcome,'
and only then realised something else: Craig thought this
was the place she had promised him, her favourite place
in the world.

It was not. But he had given her, inadvertently, the
chance to turn around and go home. Not to risk sharing
with him that other, secret place where she had never
taken anyone, not even Kathrin.

His smile deepened. 'You look so serious...this is no
time to be solving the problems of the world. What are
you thinking about, Marya?'

She tossed back her red hair and her eyes, green in
the sun, laughed at him recklessly. 'This isn't my favourite place,' she announced. 'That's still to come.'

'So were the fishermen right to be wary of a red-haired
woman?' he said softly. 'You've bewitched me...I'd
follow you to the ends of the earth.'

Her lips curved provocatively. 'You won't have to go
that far. And I promise you'll like it.'

'I have no doubt of that,' he replied, his gaze ca-
ressing the soft line of her mouth.

Her heart was beating erratically, and she was filled
with a primitive excitement. There was no going back

now, nor did she want to. As she leaned forward to row again, the scooped neck of her blouse exposed the shadowed valley between her breasts and the jut of her collarbones, and she saw Craig's eyes drop and knew what he was seeing. She held her position, the colour rising in her cheeks but her eyes fearless as a merlin's.

He said huskily, 'This is the real you, Marya...you have no idea how different you look from the first time I saw you.'

She pursed her lips and looked down her nose in exaggerated hauteur, so that he laughed out loud. 'That's it! Whatever you do, you mustn't go back to La Roulade or confine yourself in a city again. It would be like caging an eagle.'

'Or keeping a puffin in a bathtub,' she said agreeably.

His teeth very white in a wide grin, Craig hit the surface of the water with the flat of his hand, splashing her with ice-cold drops. One of them trickled down her throat to the swell of her breast, where it caught in the pleated cotton of her blouse. He said, 'If I wasn't afraid that we'd both end up in the sea, I'd kiss you right now as you've never been kissed before.'

She gave a throaty chuckle and said, 'Row, Craig. A great way to get rid of frustration.'

She bent to the oars herself, steering the boat between the finger of rock and the cliff, past two more black-mouthed caves and a long precipice to a place where the grass tumbled down the ridge, almost reaching the sea; four small islands were clustered together, humpbacked like a pod of whales. Marya headed the boat for the one furthest from the shore, the largest and steepest of the four. As they drew close Craig shipped his oars, sensing her greater knowledge of the waters.

The bow bumped gently against the rocks. Marya shucked off her sandals and, agile as a sheep, climbed out of the boat, clutching the hawswer. A rusty iron ring was embedded in the rock; she knotted the rope around it and reached out one hand. 'Can you manage?'

Craig took her hand and jumped ashore. 'You couldn't land here on a rough day.'

'It's almost never calm enough to land here—that was always one of its attractions,' she said. 'The men used to come here years ago to hunt for seabirds, but no one comes now.'

'Except you.'

The rock dug into her bare feet. She inhaled the sharp tang of seaweed and the pungency of thyme, and said, almost to herself, 'Three years can seem like forever... when things were at their worst this was the place I would remember, and somehow it would always get me through.'

Craig knelt down to examine a small rock pool, sensitive enough to leave her alone for this very private homecoming. A few moments later Marya gave a deep sigh of repletion. Then she glanced down at the man at her feet, at the long curve of his spine and the curl of hair at his nape. 'Do you want to follow me?'

He stood up with the easy grace that was so characteristic of him. She was standing close to him, a slim figure in a full skirt and a close-fitting blouse, her whole bearing radiating a kind of happiness she had never shown him before. He could have taken her in his arms. Instead he nodded and said, 'Anywhere, Marya.'

She gave a laugh as fleeting and light-hearted as a splash of foam. 'The choices aren't many. Up or into the sea.' Turning her back, she led him over the rocks towards the grass slope.

The first part of the climb was easy. But then the gradient steepened abruptly. In a flash of bare limbs Marya scaled the bank, using clumps of grass as toeholds, her fingers digging into the sparse soil. The top of the island levelled out, hedged in with rough-edged boulders that cupped the sun and provided protection from the wind, so that the grass was a carpet of pink and gold wild flowers. The sky enclosed them in a blue dome across which the fulmars and gulls soared in wide circles.

Marya turned to face her companion, and for the first time was struck by doubt. What if he didn't like it here? What if he couldn't understand why this place had been, ever since she had discovered it, a sanctuary from the rest of the world? The place that, in memory, had kept her sanity in Toronto?

She need not have worried. Without hurrying Craig let himself be absorbed in the peace of his surroundings; only then did he say, 'It's perfect, Marya—thank you for bringing me here.'

She had been right to trust her instincts and show him her island, Marya thought joyously. And, deep within her, she was glad too that he was the only one to whom she had ever given this part of herself. She stood still, waiting, the sun laving her bare arms and legs.

She was silhouetted against the rocks and sky, poised like a seabird that could take flight at any moment. Intuitively Craig did not use words. Instead he crossed the grass towards her and without haste put his arms around her, linking his fingers loosely behind her back. His kiss was an extension of the beauty of the day, his lips sun-warmed and sure of their welcome, but again without haste. There is all the time in the world, they seemed to say. Time for us to learn about each other. Time to give and time to take. Time to surrender...

Marya looped her arms around his neck, her body fitting very naturally into his, as if fashioned for him. Perhaps ever since she had discovered this little island

and claimed it for her own she had known that this would happen, that one day she would share her secret with a man. Share more than her secret. Share herself, the real woman whose core Tony had never reached.

Craig's mouth moved against hers gently at first, then more insistently, until she parted her lips and felt the dart of his tongue like fire through her body. His hands tightened in the small of her back, pulling her closer. Willingly she moulded herself into him, playing with the soft blond hair on his nape, glorying in the hard wall of his chest pressed so intimately against her breasts. She slid her hands the length of his body, her palms curving to fit the arc of his ribs and the jut of his hipbones. And still the kiss went on, until she thought she would die from the pleasure of it.

He let his mouth trail down her throat, nibbling at the soft flesh. Then, suddenly impatient, he pushed her blouse down over her shoulders and drew back from her, his eyes feasting on her swollen lips and the flare of passion in her face before moving to the creamy skin that he had bared. But still he said nothing. His features intent, he began unlacing her blouse, the brush of his hands making her tremble very lightly. The blouse, loosened, fell away from her body.

He bent his head and kissed the hollow between her breasts, then pushed aside the lace of her bra to stroke the firm, pale skin. Marya was trembling openly now, her eyes dazed with desire. She circled his waist, holding him tightly, and felt the throb and force of his arousal against her belly.

They fell apart with one accord, Craig ripping at the buttons on his shirt, Marya pulling her blouse over her head in one swift movement and throwing it to the ground. He was naked to the waist now, his chest with a tangle of hair that narrowed to his navel; she found

him very beautiful. Her hands awkward with haste, she
undid her skirt, then stepped out of it. Craig's trousers
were lying in a heap on the grass, and deliberately he
took off the narrow briefs he was wearing beneath them.

Instinctively she applauded his action, for in this wild
and lonely place how could they be anything but naked
under the sun? She slipped off her two lacy undergar-
ments and held out her hands to him.

'Marya, Marya...you're the only woman in the world
for me,' Craig said hoarsely. Then, in a reverent silence,
he traced the curves and contours of her body from
shoulder to hip before taking her hands in his and pulling
her close again for another long, drugged kiss. Slowly,
almost indolently, they lay down together on the soft
carpet of grass.

Craig made love to her as if she were indeed the only
woman in the world; as if he had never been with a
woman before, so that each movement was new and innocent and fresh in a blinding voyage of discovery. And
from him Marya caught this innocence, any remnants
of Tony vanishing from her consciousness, her own re-
sponses combining a virginal shyness with a fierce joy
in the hungers of her own body, and an equally fierce
pride in his obvious delight in her. They spoke very little,
for it was a communion far beyond words; the shine in
Marya's eyes, the wash of delicate pink in her cheeks,
the fall of sun and shadow across her body said all that
needed to be said.

When he entered her, her body arched to hold him,
her eyes as depthless as the sea. She could see the sudden
tension in his face and knew its source, for it was her
own: on the one hand the yearning to prolong this
passionate delight; on the other the drive, as old as the
land on which they lay, as inevitable as the ocean tides,
to find the completion that they sought. Craig said with

desperate honesty, 'Marya, sweetheart ... now,' and as though his voice was the only catalyst she needed she allowed the rhythms to overcome her and drown her in their spiralling intensity. From a long way away she heard her own voice join the distant cries of the seabirds.

Very slowly Marya came back to herself. She was cradled in the circle of Craig's arms, his head resting on her shoulder, his thigh thrown over hers. Her heartbeat was returning to normal. She became aware of the scent of crushed grass and of coolness on her skin, and with a piercing regret knew that her body was her own again, a separate entity to be reclaimed. Scarcely ready to acknowledge this to herself, certainly unready to tell Craig, she lay still and purposely let the security of his embrace enfold her.

It was he who finally broke the silence. He kissed her on the lips, then said, his breath fanning her cheek, 'I'm glad we made love for the first time outdoors ... you belong with the flowers and the sunshine, Marya. You're more beautiful than I can say.'

Still caught in the wonder of an intimacy greater than any she had ever known, not yet ready to examine that little phrase, the first time, she said softly, 'Was it good for you, Craig?'

'Do you even have to ask?' he murmured into her neck. Then he came up on one elbow, tracing the line of her jaw with the tip of one finger. 'Yes, it was good. Although good is a totally inadequate word.' He frowned to himself, searching for a better one. 'I felt as if I'd never been with a woman before. As though by coming to this place we'd wiped out the past...do you know what I mean?'

She nodded, almost frightened by his uncanny rapport with what she herself had felt. Cool air brushed her back, and she shivered. 'Is the wind coming up?' she asked.

As Craig got to his feet she followed suit, secretly admiring his flat belly and long, muscular legs. She could feel the breeze now and in quick alarm said, 'We'll have to go—the slightest wind can be dangerous here.'

'I don't want to leave.'

She looked at him uncertainly. 'But we must.' Managing a smile, she added, 'You really wouldn't like being marooned here.'

He said with the utmost seriousness, 'With you, I'd risk it...one more kiss, Marya.'

Marya walked into the circle of his arms again. But this time, despite the warm pressure of Craig's mouth, the kiss spoke to her of endings, not of beginnings, and again she shivered. 'You're cold,' he said. 'You'd better put some clothes on...just let me look at you once more.'

Once Tony had found his own release in the act of love, he had lost interest; Craig, she was beginning to realise, was very different. She sensed him wanting to hold on to the memory of what had happened between them, and unconsciously she tensed. The implications of their lovemaking were too immense for her to take in right away; she found herself suddenly wanting to be alone. Then she heard Craig say roughly, 'Don't look like that, Marya!'

She bent to gather her scattered clothes, hauling on her lacy underwear and then her skirt with awkward haste. 'Like what?'

'As though you're already in flight. Gone from me before I'm ready...before I'm fully aware of what's happened.'

'We made love,' she said flatly. 'That's what happened.' She reached behind her back to do up her bra, her shoulders tense, the soft flesh of her belly pulled taut. Desire flared in his eyes just as if he had never slaked it in her arms; panicking, she yanked her blouse over her head and said raggedly, 'Craig, we really have to go.'

Without the slightest self-consciousness he started putting on his own clothes, his face set in a way that boded no good. Marya tucked in her blouse and headed across the clearing to the little path down the rocks. Because she was not paying attention, she bruised her foot on a rock and scraped her knee. But the boat was at its mooring, swaying gently on waves that had not been there when they arrived. How long ago had that been? she wondered, staring at the shore, and knew that chronological time had nothing to do with their stay on the island.

As he came down the path Craig dislodged a couple of stones, which clattered over the rocks and splashed into the sea. She turned around and said briskly, 'You'd better get in first—I'll cast off.'

With a directness she might have anticipated, Craig answered, 'Marya, when I said this was the first time we'd make love, I meant it. I'm not going to disappear the way Tony did.'

'But you're a rich man!' she cried, and knew the words had been hovering just below the surface of her mind, waiting to be said.

He took her by the shoulders. 'I'm a real person!' he blazed. 'I'm not a goddamned stereotype walking into your fancy restaurant in Toronto. I'm Craig. I made love to you up there on the hill—remember?'

The wind blew a strand of hair across her face. She brushed it back and said fiercely, 'We've got to go.'

He did not release her. In a strange voice he said, 'Do you know what, Marya? I think I'm falling in love with you...maybe I already have.'

Maybe, she thought. The land of maybe. 'You don't have to say those words just to dress up what happened, Craig. To make me feel better.' Her voice was shaking; she forced it under control. 'I made love to you willingly—perhaps that's why I brought you here. But it's over now and we have to go back to the other world, where we have families and jobs and commitments. That's the real world.'

'Are you saying that what happened here today wasn't real?' he demanded furiously.

'This is a magical place...outside of normal time,' she retorted. 'You spoke of bewitchment—maybe we were both bewitched.'

'It was real, Marya. *Real!*'

She pulled free. 'We can argue all the way home if you like. But for heaven's sake get in the boat!'

His eyes like granite, Craig grasped the gunwale and climbed in, sitting on the thwart nearest the stern. Marya untied the hawser and sat near the bow, pushing away from the rocks. She began to row with ferocious energy. As Craig picked up the rhythm, the boat surged through the water, waves slapping at the prow. Foam, white as lace, edged the shore now while the gulls swooped high over the cliffs on invisible wind currents.

Rowing, by its very repetitiveness, left Marya's mind free. She had not meant to say that about rich men, she thought miserably. It had slipped out. Or were the real truths to be found in those remarks that popped out on one's tongue without conscious volition?

Craig was a rich Canadian. So was Tony. Craig and she had made love. So had she and Tony.

But it was not that simple. Agitated though she was, she could not blind herself to the differences between the two men. Craig had an inner strength and a directness Tony had lacked, and Craig had understood the magic of her island in a way Tony could not possibly have.

But Craig did not want his brother marrying her sister.

She forced her attention to the passage between the finger of rock and the cliff, the noisy complaints of the guillemots accompanying the flash of oars in the sun. Only then did she acknowledge the real truth. Rich man, poor man—that was a smokescreen. The real issue was that she was vulnerable again.

She stared at the flex and pull of the muscles in Craig's back. In the gift of his body he had paid her the twin compliments of generosity and total involvement, and in so doing had given her something of his soul. She understood now the small, soft smile on Kathrin's face.

But, she thought in sheer terror, she must not fall in love again. It was too dangerous, too painful.

Yet how could she ever forget Craig? And how would she ever make love with anyone else after such felicity?

CHAPTER EIGHT

IT TOOK Craig and Marya almost an hour to row back to the wharf, for the tide was against them and the wind had sharpened. One part of Marya was in no hurry to arrive, for she had no idea how she was to behave with Craig in the aftermath of what had been a shattering degree of intimacy. Had she made love with him on a whim, with a reckless disregard for the consequences? From the rebellion that Magnus had so often deplored in her? Or had she wanted to know if Kathrin was right and that there was more to the act of love than Tony had ever shown her? Perhaps, she thought soberly, it had been inevitable that she and Craig make love ever since that searing embrace in the ferry terminal in Bergen, that seemed so long ago. Four days, she thought. That was all.

None of the tumult of her feelings had subsided by the time the side of the boat jarred against the concrete wharf. She shipped the oars, jumped out and fastened the bow to the iron ring, this one smooth and shiny from much use.

'It's turned cold, hasn't it?' she said with an artificial smile vaguely angled in Craig's direction.

'Marya, we're not going to discuss the weather. Do you want to go to Saksun?'

It was not a question she had expected. She faltered, 'Now, you mean?'

'Why not? You want to settle this business of your father, don't you? If indeed it can be settled.'

137

She said impulsively, caught by a sudden rawness in his voice, 'What's your father like, Craig?'

He avoided her eyes. 'A strong-willed, powerful man who won't listen to me unless I just about bludgeon him over the head.'

'Oh. So we have that much in common.'

'We have more than that in common. As you well know.'

Not wanting to follow this lead, Marya asked, 'What about your mother?'

A shadow crossed Craig's face. 'She died when I was very young. Six.'

'Something else we have in common,' Marya said unwillingly. 'I was five.'

With implacable purpose Craig went on, 'I know something about fathers, Marya. And while it might seem odd to compare the millionaire owner of a Canadian forestry company to a Faroese boat-builder, your father reminds me rather too much of mine... are we going to Saksun?'

Apparently there was to be no further discussion of what had taken place on the island. Not realising quite how transparent her features were, Marya gave him a smile of all too evident relief and said, 'Lunch first? I'll make you a sandwich at Aunt Grethe's.'

'You might even make me two,' he drawled. 'I seem to have developed an appetite.'

Refusing to blush, she remarked, 'Rowing's hard work.'

'Plus all that sea air. You've got a bit of grass in your hair, Marya—hold still.'

Despite all her good intentions she could feel herself blushing as he very carefully extracted several crushed blades of grass from among her curls. 'There,' he said, 'now I think we can face your aunt. Did I do up my shirt on the right buttons?'

Marya bit her lip, remembering with embarrassing clarity exactly how he had shed his shirt. 'Is it written all over us?' she asked helplessly. 'It must be.'

'I can tell, of course. But no one else will.'

'It was my fault!' she burst out. 'I was the one who took you there.'

With a steel edge to his voice Craig said, 'Marya, fault is a horrible word. If we never as much as hold hands again, what we shared today was an incomparable gift.'

Unexpected tears filmed her eyes. 'I suppose it was,' she mumbled.

'You don't sound very sure,' he said irritably, turned on his heel and strode up the wharf.

She glared after his retreating back, stamped her sandalled foot and yelled, 'It was the most beautiful thing that's ever happened to me!'

Craig stopped dead in his tracks and pivoted to face her. She was still glaring at him, the wind teasing her hair and blowing her skirt about her legs. He strolled back to her, his hands in his pockets, and said with true amusement, 'I don't think I'd risk making love to you right now—you look as if you'd like to put a knife between my ribs. Less and less can I imagine you cooped up in an elegant restaurant and saying all the right things to the right people.' Without changing his expression he added, 'You'll like where I live, Marya, it's as wild and remote as your island.'

When she was living in Toronto Marya had seen pictures of the west coast—the spectacular snow-capped Rocky Mountains, the lush forests, and the dark blue waters of the Pacific Ocean—and had longed to go there. 'I won't have the chance to like it or dislike it,' she said shortly. 'Because I won't be going there.'

His eyes narrowed with purpose. 'Yes, you will.'

'Craig, I played that game once before.'

'But you didn't play it with me.' He gave her a lazy smile. 'Did you mention lunch? Is Grethe your mother's sister?'

'You are a very frustrating man!'

'If you're frustrated, my darling Marya, then I'm a failure as a man.'

A reluctant smile tugged at her lips; Tony, she realised with a tiny shock of surprise, had had very little sense of humour. Glad to find a safe topic among a minefield of unsafe ones, she began explaining who Grethe was as they trudged along the path to the village. 'She thinks men are marvellous creatures and that it's her mission in life to feed them,' she finished. 'Here we are.'

Grethe's kitchen smelled sweetly of apple cake and she had a dab of flour on her nose. When she was not cooking, Grethe liked to read highly coloured novels about her Viking ancestors, so big blond-haired men were her special weakness; Craig was soon seated in front of a huge slab of cake which was smothered in thick cream. Resignedly Marya helped herself, watching as homemade bread and cheese and a big mug of tea joined Craig's apple cake. He complimented Grethe on everything, ate enough to satisfy her, and did not even blink when she mentioned all the food she would be preparing for Robb and Kathrin's wedding.

He was only allowed to leave on the condition that he would come back. But finally he and Marya set off in the car, following the coast road to Hvalvík, then doubling back along the valley and the winding river that led to Saksun. The village, like Tjørnuvík, was at the end of the road, where a circle of hills descended into a huge tidal lake. The hills, their peaks now hidden in the clouds, were streaked with waterfalls, and echoed with the whistling of whimbrels and the bleating of sheep.

Marya stood by the car, wondering what to do next; the idea of accosting a total stranger about a long-ago affair now seemed so preposterous that had Craig not been with her she was almost sure she would have abandoned her quest. But Craig said calmly, 'Let's go to that red house and ask where he lives.'

At the red house they were directed to a tiny white house on the other side of the deep chasm the river had carved; from the garden monkeyflowers and forget-me-nots had spread into the neighbouring field in an orange and blue carpet. A column of smoke rose from the chimney. Her mouth dry, Marya knocked on the door.

A very tall man, as tall as Craig if his shoulders had not been stooped, opened the door; his eyes were the colour of the forget-me-nots in the garden. As they fastened themselves on Marya's face, they widened with shock. He made the sign of the cross and croaked a greeting.

In Faroese Marya said, 'Mr Nielsen, I'm Marya Hansen, daughter of Magnus and Anna Maria Hansen. This is my friend Craig Huntingdon, from Canada.'

The blue eyes barely passed over Craig. 'I would not have believed it,' he stammered, clutching the doorframe.

'I'm sorry,' she said in compunction. 'I've been told I look like my mother, but I didn't mean to startle you... May we come in?'

'Yes, yes, of course.' He ushered them into a cramped little room heated with a peat fire. The rheumy-eyed dog on the rug paid them no attention; a scarlet and green parrot sitting on the back of a chair said something so rude in Danish that Marya was glad Craig could not understand. She said hastily, 'Craig only speaks English.'

Petur Nielsen turfed a battle-scarred cat off one of the chairs, and pulled the chair nearer the fire. 'Then we will speak English,' he said, and gave her a smile that made her understand why her mother would have been attracted to him. 'I learned it years ago when I was first mate on a British freighter.'

Now that she was here, Marya found herself unable to be circumspect. She plunged into her story, telling how Magnus had always favoured Kathrin and allowed Marya very little freedom, and describing what she had learned from Mrs Rasmussen. 'You see, if my mother did have an affair with you, then I could understand why my father hated me—because I look so like her.' Abruptly she ran out of words.

Petur Neilsen said quietly, 'I didn't have an affair with her... although I would have. I wanted to marry her the first day I met her, with her hair like flame and her eyes that changed colour the way yours do. She was eighteen years old.' The cat jumped on his lap, purring asthmatically, and absently he patted it. 'But she was in love with your father, the best boat-builder on the islands... she was kind to me, but she wanted nothing of me. So I went to sea and stayed away for six years.'

He stared into the fire, an old man lost in memory. 'I came back to Tórshavn one day in September. On my third day in port I was strolling along Tórsgóta when I met your mother, she had come to town on the bus to shop. She had two daughters, she told me, and had just found out she was expecting a third child. She was even more beautiful than before. We started walking and talking, and soon we had left town and found ourselves in the hills. I told her that I still loved her, and that if she was unhappy I would take her away from her boat-builder and make her happy again...'

'Was she unhappy?' Marya asked, knowing how important a question it was.

'I don't think your father was an easy man to live with. But she loved him, she said, and she was very loyal. So again I was turned down and again I left the islands, this time for many years. When I came home, I learned she had died bearing the child she had told me about that day in Tórshavn. So I settled here, knowing she is buried just over the mountains, and here I have stayed.' His blue eyes, filled with an old sadness, came back to Marya's face. 'Many people saw us that day in Tórshavn, and saw too, I suppose, my happiness in her company. Your father was a jealous man, she told me that ... if only one person told him about our being together all day he might well have thought she had been unfaithful to him.'

'But she was not.'

'No. Not even in thought.'

Craig spoke for the first time. 'Mr Nielsen, would you come back to Tjørnuvík with us and tell Magnus what you have just told us? For Marya's sake.'

Petur looked from Marya to Craig. 'So,' he said. 'You love Marya ... just as I loved her mother.'

The parrot's claws scraped the back of the chair. Raising its crimson crest, it gave an ear-piercing screech. Marya said loudly, 'No, he doesn't.'

Craig was staring at her, a dazed expression on his face. 'Yes, I do,' he said.

As the parrot emitted another uncouth scream and Marya made an instinctive gesture of repudiation, Craig gave an incredulous laugh. 'That was why it was so wonderful on the island—because I love you. I was blind not to have seen that, Marya. Blind!'

She scowled at him. 'You think I'm after your money. And I'll never marry a rich man—never!'

Petur said mildly, 'Yes, I'll come.' As Marya's head swung round, her eyes glinting green, he added, 'Just so did Anna Maria look when I told her I loved her— are you in love with someone else, Marya Hansen?'

'No! I'm not in love with anyone,' she said violently. 'Nor is Craig.'

'You let me speak for myself,' said Craig.

He looked far more angry than loving, and she took heart from this. Turning back to Petur and determined to change the subject, she said, 'My father may not listen to you—he chased me out of the shed with an oar this morning when I tried to ask him about my mother.'

Petur sat up a little straighter, a militant light in his mild blue eyes. 'I too can handle an oar.'

'Then why don't we go?' Craig suggested.

Marya was glad to escape from the tiny living-room, a room in which Craig loomed much too large. She slipped into the back seat of the car, leaving the two men in front, and on the way Petur and Craig traded tales of their adventures in various inaccessible parts of the globe. It was another facet to Craig; she shut her mind to it just as determinedly as she had shut her mind to his declaration of love. But she could not help wondering if her mother had been attracted to Petur because Petur had been free to roam the world, while Anna Maria's world had been Tjørnuvík and babies and a man who built boats but had not understood the meaning of wanderlust.

And what of herself? What of her own wanderlust?

Sooner than she wished, Craig pulled up outside Grethe's. When Marya pointed out the boat-shed, Petur said calmly, 'I will go in alone, please.'

He got out of the car and ambled up the slope, a long-legged man with a mop of white hair and undoubted dignity. When he reached the shed he knocked on the door, walked in, and closed the door tightly behind him.

Marya said, 'Now what do we do?'

'We wait,' Craig replied.

He was gazing through the windscreen at the shed. She looked at the hair curling on the back of his neck and remembered how soft it had felt when she had buried her fingers in it. She said tightly, 'I'm going to wait by the beach.'

'Go ahead.'

He made no move to join her. So much for his words of love, she thought vengefully as she tramped between the houses and across the grass to the stone wall at the head of the beach. She perched herself on it, elbows on her knees. Tony had mouthed empty words of love to get her into his bed; Craig had made love to her and then produced a declaration of love. What was the difference?

The clear sky and the shining sea gave her no answers. She forced her mind to what might be going on in the shed, and from there drifted to thoughts of her mother; almost an hour passed before she heard Craig come up behind her. She said eagerly, 'Is Petur back?'

'No sign of him. But the shed's still standing, so I don't think they're bashing each other with oars yet... I left a note on the windscreen that we'd be waiting for him down here.' He climbed over the wall so that he was facing her, his back to the sea, and said without finesse, 'I told you on the island I thought I was falling in love with you, Marya. I was right—I *am* in love with you.'

He was unsmiling, his eyes a level, impenetrable grey. Marshalling her thoughts, Marya said evenly, 'Craig, you don't have to do this. I know we made love this morning, and probably we shouldn't have, it was a crazy, impetuous thing to do... but just because we were both overtaken by passion or lust or whatever you want to call it, you don't have to come up with a whole lot of fancy words about being undyingly in love with me...' Her voice broke. 'In fact, I'd much rather you didn't.'

His nostrils flared. 'So that's how you see it, is it? I'm appeasing my guilt? I'm trying to prettify something as elemental as the ocean with words I don't mean? Thanks for making love, Marya, I'll love you forever, and goodbye?'

'Yes,' she said coldly, 'that's how I see it.'

'I don't believe you!' he snarled. 'I know what's wrong with you—because of Tony you're terrified of those three little words, I love you. So you've decided all men are alike and, while you might occasionally go to bed with one out of lust or passion, you certainly won't let your emotions——'

'I haven't been with a man since Tony!'

'So what's so different about me?'

Digging her nails into the moss on the rocks, she cried, 'It was the place! I've always loved that island, I told you that. We mated there, Craig—like two eagles we mated, and it was beautiful and, yes, it was as elemental as the ocean. But now it's over. Don't you understand—over!'

'I won't accept that. Do you know what I was thinking about in the car before I came down here looking for you? I was picturing you at my home in British Columbia...it's not so different from here, Marya, except for the forest. I live north of Vancouver where it's still wilderness...deer eat the apples on the trees, salmon run up the river to spawn, whales blow in the sound. You'd love it. You belong there—with me.' He took a step towards her. 'I want you to marry me.'

She leaned back as far as she could without falling off the wall. 'So I'm to live in the wilderness while you go to board meetings in your pin-striped suit carrying an alligator briefcase and fire people who aren't even people to you? I'll never marry a rich man, Craig! You don't get rich being nice—rich men are rich because they put money ahead of anything else. Women are just one more possession to them, pleasant to have around, easy to deceive, simple to get rid of when a better one comes along. No, thanks.'

'That's what you think I'm like?' Craig said in a thin voice.

He seemed to have shrunk, and his eyes were appalled. Gritting her teeth, Marya forged on. 'It wasn't only Tony...over and over again at La Roulade and at the club I saw men like that. And they were all rich.'

He directed the full force of his personality on her. 'I won't get down on my knees and beg you to marry me. And I'm certainly not going through a detailed list of everything I've done the last ten years so you can decide whether or not I fit your prejudices about rich men. I can only be myself, Marya. And if that's not enough, I——'

Petur's voice hailed them from the road. Never more glad to be rescued in her life, Marya waved at him and swung her legs over the wall so she could jump to the ground. She ran across the grass and said breathlessly, 'How did you get along?'

Petur waited until Craig had joined them. 'First he tried to show me the door,' he said imperturbably. 'Once it became clear I did not wish to leave, he accused me of ruining his marriage. It was quite lively for a while.'

Knowing Magnus, Marya decided this was probably an understatement. 'So he did think my mother had been unfaithful.'

'Oh, yes. Apparently one of the neighbours made sure he knew she and I had spent the day together in

Tórshavn. And, of course, before she married Magnus I had made no secret of my feelings for her. So Magnus had put two and two together and got six.'

Wondering if the neighbour was the much-widowed Mrs Rasmussen, Marya asked the key question, 'Did he believe you, Petur?'

Petur sobered. 'Yes...after he had listened to all I had to say, he did. Which meant, of course, that *he* had ruined the last months of his marriage. Not me. Not Anna Maria. It was hard for him to accept that. Also he now realises that for many years he punished his red-haired daughter for resembling her mother. That, too, was not easy for him to acknowledge.'

'Does he want to see me?' Marya asked in a stifled voice. As Petur nodded, she took his hands in hers and reached up and kissed him on each cheek. 'Thank you, Petur. Thank you a thousand times...may I come and visit you again?'

'You may, most certainly. But you will also be seeing me here.' A twinkle in his eye, he finished, 'Magnus and I will work together on some models of old Viking ships.

Marya had to laugh. 'You accomplished a lot in a very short time.'

Craig said in a clipped voice, 'I'll drive you home, Petur, while Marya's with her father.'

Her eyes swivelled to meet his. In a lightning flash-back everything they had said and done that day passed in front of her and she flushed as vivid a scarlet as the parrot's crest. 'Thank you,' she muttered.

He gave her a curt nod. Petur, an interested spectator to all this, said without looking directly at either one of them, 'To live with regret can be bitter and lonely...goodbye, Marya.'

Rooted to the spot, she watched them walk away from her, two tall men who were changing her life. Did Craig really want to marry her? Would she regret it if, out of fear and anger, she refused to even consider his offer?

The door of the boat-shed was shut. Marya pushed it open without knocking and said, 'Hello, Pa.'

Magnus had been standing at the little window that looked towards the graveyard, his hands idle for once. For the first time in her life Marya saw him as an old man, and with a surge of compassion she crossed the room and took his hands in hers. 'It's all right,' she said forcefully. 'Mama knew you well—she would have understood.'

He spoke with painful accuracy. 'I doubted her…when I asked her if there was truth in the rumours, she laughed at me and said Petur was just a friend and they'd walked in the hills together because it was a fine day and she didn't like shopping. But I chose not to believe her…perhaps because I never quite believed that a woman as beautiful and free of spirit as Anna could love me.' His voice grew harsher. 'But Petur told me she did love me.'

'It's all right,' Marya repeated helplessly.

'And then after she died I put my anger on you, who looked so much like her…' He cleared his throat. 'I'm sorry,' he said stiffly. 'I did a great wrong.'

Knowing how difficult it had been for him to apologise, Marya put her arms around him and hugged him, feeling his initial resistance, then the tentative return of her embrace. 'You're forgiven,' she said warmly. 'It's OK, Pa.'

She let go of him before he could pull away. He ran his finger under his collar and then headed for his work-bench, picking up a chisel as if it were a familiar friend and bending to a rib he was carving. She began asking about the Viking models, and they were in the middle of what was for Magnus an animated discussion when he suddenly stopped and frowned at her across the width of the boat. 'This man who was in the house yesterday... what are his intentions?'

The words were out before she could stop them. 'He wants to marry me, Pa.'

'So—another of my daughters will be going across the sea.'

'No, I won't. I don't want to marry him.'

'He's very different from the one you left with three years ago.'

'How can I be sure of that?' she retorted spiritedly.

'He came to your defence in my own house. Would the other man have done that?'

Magnus had never liked Tony and had avoided calling him by name. 'No,' she said slowly. 'Tony wouldn't have done that.'

'Once in your life you do a stupid thing. Do you for the rest of your years do nothing in case that too is stupid?'

With sudden insight she said, 'Grethe... you might have married Grethe.'

Magnus brushed some shavings to the floor. 'Yes. But I couldn't let go of your mother, so how could I marry anyone else? Don't carry that other man for the rest of your life, Marya, as I have carried my anger.'

He was tapping the end of the chisel industriously, his wool cap pulled down over his ears even though the shed was warm. 'I'm afraid of being hurt,' Marya confessed baldly, and with part of her brain she marvelled that she should be sharing such a sentiment with her father.

'Would you rather be like the Witch and the Giant? Turned to stone at sunset?' His chisel slipped and he frowned at her peevishly. 'Tell Grethe I will be late for supper…how can a man get his work done with all these interruptions?'

With a wry grin Marya realised she could not expect Magnus to turn into a saint overnight. 'OK, Pa,' she said. Before he could duck she kissed his cheek, knocking his cap askew, and then ran from the shed.

CHAPTER NINE

KATHRIN was not working the next day, so she and Robb were taking a picnic up into the hills. Grethe had gone to Tórshavn to shop; the men and boys of Tjørnuvík were helping at a round-up in Haldarsvík, so the village felt deserted; and there was no sign of Craig. Marya, in jeans and a sweater, was sitting in Grethe's kitchen watching her sister make sandwiches when Robb arrived.

Now that Marya knew him better, she was able to see the ways Robb resembled his brother: the line of his jaw, the way he tilted his head, the shape of his hands. The lean fingers with their well-kept nails could have been Craig's. Fingers that had explored all the intimacies of her body...

'Are you all right, Marya?' Kathrin asked curiously.

'Sure—I'm fine.' She gave Robb an unconvincing smile. 'I thought Craig might have come with you.'

'When I went in to say good morning, he turned over in bed, growled something about being awake all night, and went back to sleep. Not like him—he's usually up with the birds.'

Marya had not slept well either, and at one point had woken from a highly erotic dream reaching out for Craig in the darkness. Noticing that Kathrin and Robb were both staring at her, she jumped to her feet. 'I'll fill the Thermos,' she said, and suited action to the word, making a lot of unnecessary noise as she did so.

Robb said easily, 'Too bad he hadn't come. The four of us could have gone together.'

'So he's accepted the idea of your marriage?' Marya blurted.

'I wouldn't go that far. But at least he's stopped treating me like a sixteen-year-old.'

'He smiled at me the other day,' Kathrin said insouciantly.

He had smiled at Marya yesterday, when she was lying in the circle of his arms after they had made love. With a chill of fear she wondered if she would ever lie with him again.

Glancing quickly at Robb, Kathrin said, 'Why don't you come with us, Marya? It would do you good.'

'Oh, no, thanks. I'm fine,' Marya repeated, and thought if she said it often enough it might come true. She added milk to the tea and fastened the cap. 'There you go.'

Kathrin placed what was quite a substantial picnic in Robb's haversack, adding two rainjackets and looping a sweater around her neck. 'Ready?' she asked Robb with a bright smile.

He kissed her on the tip of her nose. 'Ready.'

The kitchen seemed much smaller when they had gone, and very empty. Marya went back to Magnus's, cleaned out all the cupboards in the kitchen and scrubbed the floor, then went over to Grethe's to have a bath. She should have been happy, she thought, sloshing the water back and forth along her body. Kathrin had forgiven her. Magnus and she were well on the way to being reconciled. And she had discovered that the act of love could indeed shake the soul, as the poets had promised. So why was she so out of sorts, so filled with unease?

She dried herself, got dressed, ate some bread and cheese and wandered outside. The river rattled the stones in its bed and the pony whickered a greeting. She fed it some choice clumps of grass, stroking its silky nose, then followed the river up the hill to where it spurted over the rocks in a series of miniature waterfalls. The water was cold, numbing her fingers...

She glanced down at the village and saw a tall, tawny-haired man climbing the slope towards her.

Her heart leaped in her breast, piercing her with a shaft of pure happiness. He had come. He had sought her out.

Waving at him, she called out a cheerful greeting. But Craig was jumping from rock to rock and did not reply. When he reached her, he stationed himself on a couple of boulders, one knee bent, arms resting across his thighs, and regarded her soberly. He did not, Marya thought, look particularly pleased to see her.

Not one to refuse a challenge, she said blithely, 'You look as though you got out of bed the wrong side.'

'The only thing wrong with my bed was that you weren't in it.'

'Eagles don't mate in beds,' she said primly.

'No. But ordinary people do. Real people. Even rich people.'

'Kathrin and Robb are spending the day together,' Marya remarked, indicating the long sweep of the hill behind them with a graceful gesture. 'Back that way. Just in case you were thinking of waving your money in front of her nose.'

Neither her grace nor her composure appeared to impress him. 'I didn't come here to talk about Kathrin and Robb. I came here to talk about us.'

His mouth was an uncompromising line. Marya regarded it thoughtfully. 'Maybe I don't want to talk about us,' she said.

'If you try to run away I'll stop you. Short of stuffing your ears with grass, you're caught.'

She backed off a couple of steps, calculating the distance she would have to swerve to avoid him, wishing she had something on her feet other than her old leather thongs. He straightened, his eyes trained on her face. 'So it's run, is it?' he said softly. 'That's one of the things I like about you ... you have a penchant for the interesting and the unexpected.'

'Would you rather I fall at your feet weeping for mercy?'

'I have difficulty picturing it. Marya, after a very long and sleepless night, I still want to marry you.'

She picked up a handful of wet stones, fired them in Craig's direction and took off in a fast run at an angle down the hillside. Moving so quickly that his big body was a blur, Craig leaped in front of her and caught her around the waist, pulling her hard against his chest so that the breath was driven out of her lungs. For a moment she had to cling to him to keep her balance, her hair a glossy swirl of colour on his shoulder.

Then, fighting for air, Marya pushed herself away. By no means all her breathlessness was due to the way her ribs had thudded into his; some of it came from more earthy sources, not unrelated to the racing pulse at the base of her throat and the remembered warmth of his skin. She said, her eyes grass-green, 'He-man stuff. The supremacy of the male depends on a larger skeletal frame.' With wicked deliberation she smoothed her fingers across the width of one shoulder. 'And a more highly developed musculature,' she added.

'I'm the Giant and you're the Witch,' he said amiably. 'If you keep that up, Marya, you're going to find yourself flat on your back in the grass.'

'In full view of the village?' she countered, batting her lashes.

'I will admit to you, probably unwisely, that long brown lashes and big green eyes are weapons every bit as effective as any skeletal frame. In consequence, I am embarrassingly ready to ravish you in the grass.' He stepped back, holding her at arm's length. 'Marry me, Marya.'

Marya had been quite aware of his readiness to ravish her and of her own to be ravished. She said with admirable aplomb, 'That sounds like the first line of a not very good song...marry me, Marya, oh, marry me, do. No, thank you, Craig.'

The smile faded from his face. 'If I were a poor New Zealander instead of a rich Canadian, would you marry me?'

'You're not. Next question?'

He dropped his arms to his sides. 'Look, let's quit fooling around. I got a phone call yesterday from Vancouver. There are some developments in my line of work that I don't like the sound of at all, and it could mean that I'll have to go home to straighten things out. If it weren't something crucial that I've been leading up to for the last three years, I'd say to hell with it. But it is crucial...it puts everything I've been striving for on the line and I can't afford to let it slip.'

His words had filled Marya with cold fear. She lashed, 'Can't afford? With all your money?'

His voice hardened. 'This, oddly enough, is not a question of money. If you——' Suddenly he turned his head. 'What was that?'

'I didn't hear anything.' He might be leaving...going back to Canada. He had made love to her, and now he was leaving...

'I thought I heard someone calling—there it is again.'

This time Marya heard it as well, the rise and fall of a human voice in distress. Narrowing her eyes against the light, she searched the hillside. 'Up there! By the outcrop of rock to the right...someone's running.' Her attention sharpened. 'It's Kathrin!'

Not waiting for Craig's response, she started to run herself, cutting across the hill on a diagonal path that would intersect with her sister's. 'They went for a picnic, she and Robb,' she threw over her shoulder at the man jogging behind her. 'Something must have gone wrong.'

'I don't see Robb,' Craig said grimly, and began running faster in long, smooth strides that ate up the distance.

Kathrin was closer now, dashing pell-mell down the hill, her arms and legs flailing the air as if she had been running for a long time and was very tired. 'She'll fall if she keeps that up,' Marya gasped.

'I'll go ahead and meet her.'

His strides lengthened. He was climbing all the time, altering course so Kathrin would meet him. Marya, impeded by her thongs, ran after him as fast as she could, and saw Kathrin collapse into his arms. She sensed his urgent question, and as she finally reached them heard Kathrin sob, 'It's Robb, it's Robb...'

Kathrin's eyes were glazed with exhaustion and fear, her whole body shaking. Craig said with a calmness belied by the anxiety in his eyes, 'Take a minute to get your breath...is he hurt?'

For a moment Kathrin rested her blonde curls on Craig's chest, struggling to control her breathing. 'He fell—he knocked himself out,' she panted. 'We were up by the puffin cliffs and a sheep had fallen on to one of the ledges and couldn't go up or down...the poor thing was bleating and Robb thought he could rescue it. I told him not to, that we should go for help in the village, but he wouldn't listen.'

'So I suppose he took off down the cliff without a rope and that's how he fell,' Craig put in, sounding very much like an older brother.

'H-he landed on the ledge and banged his head on a rock.' Her big blue eyes drowned in tears, Kathrin wailed, 'I could see blood—and I had to leave him there all alone.'

'He always was a pushover for an animal,' Craig rasped. 'We'd better go and get some rope and a stretcher. How far away is he, Kathrin?'

'About three miles. We've got to hurry!' She glared at Craig's set face, behind which Marya suspected he was thinking furiously. 'You don't even look as though you *care*.'

'Of course I do,' Craig retorted. 'But you've got to admit he'd have been better off listening to you...we can get help in the village, can't we, Marya?'

Marya's face fell. 'All the men are in Haldarsvík at the round-up.'

'Then we'll manage on our own. Can we get some rope?'

'There's an emergency kit near the wharf. A stretcher, too.'

'OK. Kathrin, you stay here—you're exhausted. Marya and I will get what we need and be back here as fast as we can.'

'Do *hurry*,' Kathrin pleaded.

Marya gave her sister a quick hug. 'We won't be long.' Then as Craig began running down the hill, she dashed after him.

They ran all the way to the wharf, by which time Marya had decided that a year at La Roulade had not left her in the best of shape. Panting, she unlatched the door of the little emergency hut, where Craig assessed the coils of rope neatly hanging on the far wall, and the pitons arranged in a heap by the door. Making his selection, he nodded approvingly as Marya picked up a collapsible stretcher and the first-aid kit. 'That should do it,' he said.

It was the first time he had spoken since they had left Kathrin; not waiting for a reply, he headed for the door. She hurried after him, made him wait while she got more serviceable footware from her room, and then ran with him through the houses to the river, where they started climbing again, weighed down by their equipment.

When they reached Kathrin they did not get any thanks for their speed. 'What took you so long?' she cried, and began bounding up the hillside.

Doggedly Marya followed. By the time they had traced the riverbed to the top of the hill and scrambled over the last outcrop of basalt, she had come to the conclusion that Craig, unlike her, was as fit as an athlete. As he reached back a hand to haul her up the rock face, she swallowed her pride and allowed herself to be helped.

The ground was more level now. Kathrin darted ahead across the rock-strewn plateau; Craig, burdened with the metal pitons, jogged after her. Marya brought up the rear. Craig might be at home in the boardroom in a pin-striped suit, she thought through the pain in her chest, but he was equally competent on the bare hills of her homeland.

They had passed the steep cliffs where the guillemots roosted, and still Kathrin kept running. By now Marya knew where she was headed: a sheltered, flower-strewn hollow overlooking a little cove, a place the two girls used to visit to make daisy chains and while away the summer afternoons. There had been ledges overlooking the cove, she remembered, and with a cold clench in her stomach remembered too how the water would slosh at the base of the ledges and the seaweed would writhe in the waves. She made a valiant effort to catch up with the others, her wrists aching from the weight of the stretcher.

Five minutes later they arrived. Kathrin fell on her knees at the edge of the cliff, and as Craig and Marya crowded behind her she cried out, 'Robb—oh, Robb, you're not dead!'

'No,' said Robb, who was standing upright on a ledge no more than three feet wide and was smiling at her rather unsteadily. He added urgently, 'Are you all right, Kat?'

'Fine,' she quavered, scrubbing at the tears that were pouring down her cheeks. 'I'm crying because I'm so relieved—I thought you might have fallen off the ledge and drowned.'

The sheep, a scruffy chestnut ewe, pointed her nose to the sky and baaed a pathetic appeal. Marya, overcome with relief at finding her future brother-in-law very much alive, and overcome at a more mundane level by physical exertion, sat down on the nearest clump of grass. 'Now what?' she said.

Robb grinned at her. His shirt and jeans were streaked with dirt, and blood had dried in a theatrical smear down the left side of his face. He said drily, 'I would suspect a brotherly lecture might be next on the agenda.'

'I'll save it,' Craig replied. He was testing the ground with the pitons, his face intent on his task; with a certainty that took her by surprise, so strong was it, Marya knew that if she were in Robb's position she would trust Craig absolutely. She watched in silence as he anchored the metal picks, looped rope through them, and tied a number of intricate knots with fingers that never once hesitated. The first time she had seen him, she thought, she had pictured him as a mountain climber; it would seem she had not been far wrong.

Two rope ends slithered across the rock and down the face of the cliff, coming to rest at Robb's feet. 'Robb,' Craig said, his face very serious, 'if you're feeling as lousy as you look, forget the sheep. We'll bring you up first and worry about her afterwards.'

'Sheep first,' said Robb.

Craig nodded, unsurprised. 'Get the rope around her as best you can, then.'

The ledge was narrow and the sheep uncooperative; but several interesting minutes later the animal was trussed in a rough harness. 'Marya, Kathrin, can you lend a hand?' Craig asked, positioning them in front of him. 'Pull when I tell you to...*now*.'

Marya pulled with all her strength, the ropes biting into her palms as she helped to take the animal's weight. The ewe set up a hideous complaining as her hoofs left the illusory safety of the ledge and Robb yelled up, 'You're doing fine!'

The ewe's face appeared, eyes rolling in terror, her black-pointed hoofs scrabbling for purchase in the ground. As she got to her feet and shook herself indignantly, the rope suddenly slackened and Marya landed on her behind in the grass; despite Robb's predicament, she had a strong urge to giggle. Craig ran forward, stooping to extricate the sheep from the harness, a process the sheep neither understood nor appreciated; as he wrestled with the knots he muttered a couple of words under his breath that Marya pretended not to hear. Finally the ewe freed herself from the last loop. She ran straight at Craig, knocking him flat, and kept on running until she was out of sight over a bluff.

'It was a pleasure,' Craig yelled after her. 'Any time.'

'Little Lamb, who made thee...?' Marya murmured, no longer bothering to smother her giggles.

He sat up; he was rubbing a rope burn on his thumb.
'Getting Robb up will be a picnic after that,' he said
darkly.

But Robb was unexpectedly heavy and Marya's arms
were aching with strain by the time his head and arms
reached up over the bank. Then he had heaved his torso
on to the ground, and finally his legs. For a moment he
lay still, his forehead resting on his outstretched arm,
the rope still fastened around his upper body. The back
of his shirt was as dirty as the front. Kathrin fell on her
knees beside him, wringing her hands. 'Robb, are you
all right? Robb, speak to me . . . Robb?'

He looked up at her, a look so full of love that Marya's
eyes skidded away, for such an intensity of emotion
should be private. He said, 'Kathrin, I love you . . . and
I was a fool not to listen to you. You were right, we
should have gone for help. Please don't cry.'

He got to his feet, Kathrin helping him up and clinging
to his arm; his face was very pale. With a shaky grin he
added, 'Thanks, Craig.'

Craig said calmly, 'This seems as good a moment as
any to offer both of you my apologies. If this escapade
has accomplished anything, it's shown me that money's
got nothing to do with the way you feel about each other.
I'm sorry I ever thought otherwise . . . and more sorry
that I said so. I misjudged both of you.'

There was a small silence. Then Craig and Robb
slapped each other on the back and Kathrin threw her
arms around Craig and hugged him. Marya, feeling an
outsider, bent down and fumbled with a knot in the rope;
there was a lump in her throat, for Craig's apology had
been both generous and sincere. Scowling to herself as
she broke a fingernail, she mentally added two more
qualities to her knowledge of him: competence in emer-

gencies and, far more significant, the ability to admit he had made a mistake.

Not like Tony, whispered a little voice in her ear. Tony ran from his mistakes. You being one of them.

Not like your stereotypical rich man, either.

'This is the way you undo it,' Craig said in an amused voice.

Startled, Marya looked up. He was kneeling very close to her on the ground, too close for her peace of mind. She watched as he made a couple of passes with the rope and the knot miraculously disappeared. 'I see,' she said with patent untruth, and edged away from him.

His jaw tightened and for a moment she thought he was going to say something. Instead he braced himself to haul the piton out of the ground, his grey eyes as hard as the rocks under his boots.

She dragged her eyes away from the fascinating interplay of muscles in his taut wrists, saw that Kathrin and Robb were now locked in each other's arms, and knew with horrible clarity that the predominant emotion this embrace evoked was envy. She envied Kathrin, for Kathrin knew she loved Robb, and knew too that she was loved in return.

How very simple, she thought, scrambling to her feet. The only thing she knew for sure was that she desired Craig with a shameful fervour. His hints that he might have to leave the Faroes she had pushed far to the back of her mind; she still had no idea why he had asked her to marry him, and her own feelings for him were as much a mystery.

Robb, although obviously shaken by his experience, insisted on bypassing the stretcher. They set off across the plateau, Kathrin on one side of him and Craig, looped about with rope, on the other. Marya trailed behind, lugging the stretcher and the picnic basket, and feeling totally out of sorts.

When they reached the village both Craig and Kathrin insisted on Robb's going to the hospital in Tórshavn for a check-up; Craig's voice was not one with which Marya would have cared to argue. He got in the driver's seat and said to her through the open window, 'You'll come, Marya?'

She shook her head, indicating the pile of equipment at her feet. 'I'd better put this stuff back.'

It was an impeccable excuse, as they both knew. Craig gave her an ironic smile and said, 'I'll see you when I bring Kathrin home, then.'

Maybe, thought Marya, and trudged off in the direction of the wharf to return the stretcher, the rope and the first-aid kit. Grethe was home from Tórshavn, presiding over a pot of mutton stew, and had to be told the whole story; and then the story had to be repeated for Magnus's benefit when he walked over for his dinner. Magnus was feeling sociable, and insisted Marya stay for a game of cards; she was not averse to this, feeling there might be safety in numbers should Craig seek her out.

It was nearly eight o'clock before she heard the slam of a car door outside, and then the quick tap of footsteps coming up the stairs. Kathrin burst in the room, her eyes flying to Marya's. 'Craig has to talk to you,' she announced with unconscious drama.

Marya stayed where she was, sorting her cards into suits. 'How's Robb?'

'He has a headache and a minor concussion—he's back at the hotel, resting. Marya, Craig's waiting!'

Ignoring the appeal in Kathrin's big blue eyes, Marya said stubbornly. 'He can come in if he wants to talk to me.'

'He's in a hurry—go along!'

Plainly Marya was to get no peace until she went outside. 'You can play my hand, then,' she said with rather poor grace. 'I won't be long.'

Kathrin pulled a very expressive face and said threateningly as she sat down in her sister's chair, 'Be nice to him.'

Marya tossed her head, went outside and clumped down the stairs. Craig was still sitting in the car, his fingers tapping rhythmically on the steering-wheel. He had changed his clothes, she noticed as she got in beside him. She said coolly, 'Kathrin said you wanted to talk to me?'

'Marya, I've got to leave tonight,' he said abruptly. 'There was a message waiting for me at the hotel, they've been trying to reach me since this morning. So I called the airport and they're holding the flight for me...I shouldn't have come here at all, but I had to see you.'

He had made love to her and now he was leaving. History repeating itself. Marya fumbled for the door-handle with a hand that was shaking, and said in a voice that she dimly recognised as her own, 'Goodbye—I hope you have a safe journey.'

His hand snaked out and caught her other wrist. 'Don't! I know what you're thinking, you're thinking I'm just like Tony—it's written all over your face. I'm *sorry* I've got to go, the timing's atrocious—but once this business is sorted out I'll be back on the first plane, I promise you that.'

'Craig,' she said painfully, 'please don't play games. So you're leaving. So leave. You don't have to pretend you don't want to go. And you don't have to hold out promises that one day you'll come back. In fact, I'd much rather you didn't.' She had found the handle.

Pushing against it, tugging at his hold on her wrist, she finished, 'I appreciate your saying goodbye.'

He replied with icy calm, 'You haven't been listening—I haven't yet mentioned the word goodbye.'

'You'd better—unless you want to miss your plane.' Again she tugged at her wrist. 'Let *go*!'

Sounding thoroughly angry, Craig said, 'I'll let go on one condition—if you'll promise for the space of five whole minutes to listen to me and drop all your preconceived notions about rich men.'

From his fingers through her wrist to the rest of her body physical awareness flowed like a current of electricity. She said, since it was useless to deny it, 'Craig, for some unknown reason we just have to touch each other and the earth moves. Fine. That's a fact. But you don't have to dress it up with offers of marriage and fancy speeches.'

'Listen to me!' he thundered.

Her jaw gaped, her eyes as alarmed as those of the ewe. 'You don't have to shout, either,' she said lamely.

'If it's the only way I can get your attention, I'll bellow at the top of my lungs! Now, are you listening? Or are you just waiting until I stop talking so you can jump in with fifty more arguments?'

'I'm listening,' Marya said grudgingly.

'Good.' He dropped her wrist. 'Point number one: when I first saw you at the airport in Toronto, I thought you were everything I most disliked in a woman.' As her eyes widened, he gave her an unpleasant smile. 'Took you by surprise, did I? In Toronto you looked expensive, brittle, urban to the extreme. Not my type. Point number two: since then I've found out about Tony and La Roulade and the very real struggle of a proud and courageous woman to survive. I understand, in other words, where that woman at the airport was coming from. Point number three, and remember what you said about listening: somehow over those three years you got yourself locked into a certain mind-set...probably because you didn't have the time or energy to realise what was happening. Because of what one man did, you've decided not to trust any of them, and if they're rich, forget it. Rich equals bad in your books.'

Marya turned her head away, presenting Craig with a resistant profile and hands clenched in her lap. He said relentlessly, 'You promised to listen. Anyway, this is the last thing I've got to say. When we made love on the island, I discovered the woman of passion buried underneath that other woman—the real woman, the one who grew up on a faraway island and who loves the sea and who doesn't give a fig for money or position. She's there, Marya—you've just got to set her free again.'

'Are you finished?' Marya asked with dangerous calm.

Out of the corner of her eye she saw how Craig was gripping the wheel, his skin taut over his knuckles. 'Not quite,' he said, and suddenly did not sound nearly so sure of himself. He looked over at her, his eyes tormented. 'I love you—the real you. I want to marry you.'

Instinctively Marya shrank away from him. He flinched, and almost visibly paused to regroup his forces. 'All right, maybe I'm rushing you. We have, after all, only known each other for seven days...although that's hard to believe. Marya, I'd like to come back here once my business is finished, to spend more time with you so we can get to know each other better.'

'You won't come back,' she said.

Craig looked full at her, and the first intimation of defeat hovered in his face. 'You really believe that, don't you?' As she nodded, not quite sure she could trust her voice, he went on in despair, 'I can climb mountains, rescue sheep from cliffs, take on national corporations and face hostile politicians . . . yet one red-haired woman can confound me utterly. Make everything else meaningless.'

She steeled her heart against him, fighting back the impulse to take him in her arms and soothe the tension from his face and body. She said tonelessly, 'Craig, you'll miss your plane.'

'And is that all you've got to say?'

'That's all.' The words seemed to come from nowhere and bear no relation to the turmoil within.

'Well,' Craig said. 'I guess that's that, then. There's no point in my coming back here if you don't want to see me——'

'What about Robb and Kathrin's wedding?' she flashed.

He gave a bark of unamused laughter. 'Oh, I'll probably wave a million-dollar bill in front of them and promise them a fancy wedding in Vancouver. That way *you* can make the choice of whether or not to go.'

For a moment emotion flared in Marya's chameleon eyes. But as it vanished as quickly as it had appeared, Craig said in an almost conversational voice, 'Do you know what's the worst thing about all this? The way you haven't argued with me. I'd have felt better—felt there was some hope—if you'd been yelling at me. Losing your temper. But, no. You don't even care enough to fight, do you, Marya?'

And what was she to say to that? 'Goodbye, Craig,' she replied.

'The fishermen were right . . . a red-haired woman spells danger.' Staring straight ahead of him, he said quietly, 'Goodbye, Marya.'

Marya got out of the car, slammed the door and ran for the steps. For the space of perhaps ten seconds Craig stayed hunched over the wheel, his pose filling her with an unbearable level of emotion. Then he straightened, reached for the ignition and drove off without a backward look.

What have I done? she thought in utter terror. What in God's name have I done?

CHAPTER TEN

FIVE minutes later Marya was still standing outside, huddled into the wall. Craig, she had realised through a haze of numbness, had used all his powers of persuasion and logic to make her see reason; what he had not done was to use the one weapon he could have been almost sure would have worked: his body. That he had refrained from doing so made her want to weep.

When Kathrin opened the door she saw Marya immediately, and came down the steps towards her. 'Has he——?' She peered into her sister's face. 'What's wrong? You look awful.'

'He's gone.'

'Well, of course, he had to catch the plane. But he'll be back.' Kathrin now looked rather pleased with Marya's reaction. 'You'll miss him, I expect, but——'

'No, he won't.'

'Won't what?'

'Won't be back. Ever.' Marya shuddered at the finality of her own words.

Kathrin stared at her sister in silence. Then she said incredulously, 'You turned him down.' Marya's chestnut hair fell forward to hide her face as she nodded. 'Oh, Marya, why? He's perfect for you!'

Marya told the simple truth. 'I was scared. I can't bear the thought of being vulnerable again. Of getting hurt.'

'It looks to me as though you're hurting pretty badly right now,' Kathrin said tartly.

'Better now than for the next three years.'

'You're impossible! Craig and Tony are as different as—as a hawk and a starling,' Kathrin snorted. She grimaced at her sister. 'Even so, I suppose you can't stay out here on the step for the rest of the night. Come in, and I'll make you some tea.'

Knowing she could not face either Grethe's kindness or her father's judgemental eye, Marya mumbled, 'I'm going home to bed.'

'You could call the airport and leave a message for him,' Kathrin offered hopefully.

Marya shook her head. 'Don't . . . please.'

Impulsively Kathrin hugged her. 'It will be all right, you'll see,' she said with the optimism of one who was happily in love. 'I'll be over later.'

Marya crossed the road and entered her father's empty house. In the bedroom under the eaves she undressed and got into bed. Then she lay rigidly on her back, tracing in her mind's eye the route Craig would be taking in the car. Down the coast to Kollafjørður. West to Kvívík with its Viking longhouses overlooking the sea. North to the puffin cliffs at Vestmanna and the ferry to Vágar. The drive across country, past the great waterfall called Bøsdalafossur to the runways and the modern new terminal building of the airport, where the plane would be waiting for him. Then take-off, and the long swoop up the fjord at Sørvágur past the mist-wreathed peaks of the island of Mykines, most westerly island of the Faroes . . .

She realised she was crying, slow, difficult tears that stung her eyes. Turning on her stomach, burying her face in the pillow, she let the silent tears flow; when Kathrin came to bed an hour later, she pretended to be asleep.

When Tony had left her in the luxury hotel in Toronto, Marya had had no time to grieve: survival had been her first and overriding concern. But now, with Craig gone, she had far too much time. Kathrin was working and spent most of her free hours with Robb. Marya could only clean out Magnus's cupboards so often, and Grethe, for all her kindness, basically preferred her kitchen to herself. And although Magnus now exhibited towards his elder daughter a gruff and clumsy love, he was essentially a man who preferred his own company to anyone else's.

So Marya was left to her own devices, which, as the days of the brief Faroese summer passed one by one, seemed all too often to mean that she thought about Craig.

He was with her everywhere she went. On the hills that she had roamed since a child, he accompanied her with his long-legged stride and his keen eye for beauty. When she started knitting in the evenings, to give herself something constructive to do, she saw his nimble fingers on the knotted rope at the edge of the cliff. She could not bear to go near the wharf, or the boat called *Kathrin*, and she had blanked the island out of her memory.

It was worst at night, for then his body visited her, and she would feel under her palm the smooth slide of his shoulder and the roughness of hair on his chest, and see again the grey eyes drowned in emotion as he lost himself in her.

Because she was not sleeping well she looked perpetually tired, and because she had no appetite she lost weight. Two weeks after Craig's departure Kathrin accidentally bumped into her in the kitchen at Magnus's; her arms around her sister, Kathrin said in a shocked voice, 'Marya, you're wasting away.'

Marya pulled free. 'I'm all right.'

Kathrin put her hands on her hips and announced, 'This has gone on long enough. Tonight you'll come to dinner with Robb and me at the hotel in Eiði, and you'll sit there until you eat every bite on your plate.'

Marya had been assiduously avoiding Robb and Kathrin, partly because Robb was Craig's brother, and partly because witnessing their happiness together hurt too much. 'I'm going to wash my hair this evening.'

'You can do that this afternoon.'

Marya had not been near the hotel in Eiði since the summer she had worked there as a waitress and met Tony. She said, her forehead creasing, 'Do you know, Kathrin, I can think about Tony now and it doesn't mean a thing? That's strange...'

Kathrin, who could be quite merciless when she chose, said, 'Can you do the same with Craig?'

Marya visibly flinched. 'No,' she answered in a low voice.

'When are you going to admit to yourself that you love that man?' Kathrin demanded. 'When you end up in hospital with malnutrition?'

'I don't. I——'

'I'd hate to see the way you'd behave if you did,' Kathrin retorted.

'I can't possibly——'

'You're going to sit down tonight,' Kathrin ruthlessly interrupted, 'and you're going to listen while Robb tells you some home truths about Craig and his father and his job.'

Craig had also told her to listen. 'I wish——'

'And you're going to finish up with the dessert that has the most calories on the menu,' Kathrin finished triumphantly.

'I do wish you'd stop interrupting!' Marya exclaimed.

'Goodness—a reaction out of you,' her sister said pertly. 'And promise me one thing...while you're washing your hair, you'll think about your feelings for Craig—try and figure them out. OK?'

'Oh, go away,' Marya said crossly.

But there was a little colour in her cheeks. Kathrin gave a satisfied smile, looked at her watch, shrieked, 'I'm late for work!' and ran from the kitchen.

Marya made herself a cup of tea and sat at the kitchen window in the sun to drink it. Both Craig and Kathrin had told her to listen; Craig had also told her to get rid of all her preconceived notions. Cupping her hands around her mug, feeling the sun warm her skin like the gentle touch of a hand, she deliberately emptied her mind and then allowed it to fill with thoughts of Craig. His burning grey eyes. His body, that had brought her such ecstasy. His demands on her.

Quite clearly now she could see Tony for what he was: a shallow man of the present moment, who loved only himself. In contrast Craig had a strength and integrity in which she could trust, and an uncompromising honesty which, while she had not liked it because it would not allow her to stay living in the past, had in effect jolted her from a destructive three-year pattern.

And she, she thought in horror, had likened Craig to Tony because each happened to be rich. How could she have been so blind? So unbelievably stupid?

She sat for a long time, until her tea was cold and the sun had shifted, leaving her in shadow. But she was oblivious to all this, for she was surrounded by and absorbed in her memories of Craig, losing herself in an emotion that without fanfare or surprise she knew to be love. She did love Craig; Kathrin had been right. She loved him as inevitably as the tides rose and fell, as naturally as the wild birds mated on the cliffs...

The pensive smile on her face, the look of peace, were still in place when Magnus came in looking for a lunch she had forgotten to prepare. Over the rush of water as he filled the kettle, he said, 'You look different.'

With the first proper smile she had given him since Craig had left, she said, 'I'm in love, Pa.'

'Who with?'

'Craig, of course.'

'The one you sent away two weeks ago? Funny way of showing you're in love with someone.'

The smile was wiped from her face. She *had* sent Craig away; out of fear she had driven him from her side. She had been in danger of forgetting that. 'Maybe he'll come back,' she faltered.

'Not him,' said Magnus. 'Is this the last loaf of bread?'

'Then I'll write to him,' she said defiantly. 'There's another loaf right in front of your nose, Pa.'

'So there is. It'll have to be quite a letter,' Magnus said.

So the first question Marya asked Robb when they had ordered their meal in the little hotel overlooking the clustered red and green roofs and the peaceful harbour of Eiði was, 'May I have your brother's address, Robb?'

'I can give you his home address, sure. But it's not likely he'll be there.'

'Does he stay in Vancouver when he's got board meetings?'

Robb gave her a curious look. 'What exactly has Craig told you about his job?'

Marya flushed painfully. Nothing, she thought, because she had never asked. 'Tell me about it.'

'He founded and heads up an extremely active, and to some people, highly unpopular environmental concern.'

She said blankly, 'I thought he worked for your father. Northwest Forestry.'

'He used to. But now his environmental group very frequently works against Dad. A fight they've both come to enjoy, although it certainly wasn't always that way. The reason Craig had to go home in such a hurry was to be in on the court proceedings to protect a huge valley in northern British Columbia that's threatened with clear-cutting—a whole ecosystem would be destroyed. Not by Dad's company, this time. Dad's actually getting more aware of some of the consequences of the logging industry.'

This information should not have surprised Marya, for it dovetailed perfectly with her impression of Craig. 'Couldn't I reach him by phone?' she persisted.

'Look, one day he's in court, the next day he's taking a bushplane up north, the day after he's at a rally in some little logging community—he doesn't sit in beautifully furnished boardrooms in a pin-striped suit.'

Robb could have been quoting some of her own remarks to Craig. 'I misjudged him terribly,' Marya said, her face a study in dismay. 'How am I ever going to tell him so?'

'Sooner or later he'll be in touch with me,' Robb replied, adding with some reluctance, 'His work can be dangerous, too. We're talking big money here, and some of these companies aren't too scrupulous in their methods.'

Marya had an instant and terrifying vision of Craig in his old grey cords surrounded by a dozen rough-clad men with clenched fists, who were drawing a tighter and tighter circle around him. 'Will he be phoning you?' she whispered, white-faced.

'He usually does. He's not in reach of a phone a lot of the time, of course.'

'When he does, please tell him I made a mistake to send him away,' she said. 'Tell him I'm sorry.'

'Sure,' said Robb. 'Don't look so upset, Marya—Craig's a big boy and he's been looking after himself for a long time.' He went on to describe the monumental struggle between Craig and his father, Craig refusing to be pigeonholed as the son of the boss in a company that paid only lip service to the environment, and before she knew it Marya had come to a chocolate rum torte and coffee slathered in cream. Despite all this caffeine she slept better that night than she had since Craig had left; for sooner or later Craig would get her message. He would understand that she had changed her mind and wanted to see him again . . . wouldn't he?

Four days passed, days in which Marya waited for some sign from Kathrin that Robb had talked to Craig. 'No call yet,' Kathrin would say, her blue eyes full of sympathy, and Marya would pick up her knitting—which was now to be a sweater for Craig—and concentrate on the complicated pattern.

At eight o'clock one morning, when Marya was cooking Magnus a breakfast of guillemot eggs and Kathrin was racing around getting ready for work, a knock came at the door. Mrs Rasmussen's grandson Sonni, aged seven, stood on the step, his eyes big with the importance of his task. 'There's a telephone call,' he said. 'At my gran's. For her.' He indicated Marya with a dirty finger.

'For me?' Marya repeated, and felt her heart begin to thump.

'That's right. All the way from Canada.'

'It must be Craig!' Kathrin cried. 'Hurry up, Marya . . . I'll finish Pa's eggs.'

Marya stared unseeingly at the orange centres of the eggs, her muscles paralysed. 'Do you think it is Craig?'

'I'm quite sure it's not Tony . . . go *on*, Marya.'

So Marya went, running between the houses in her bare feet and her grey robe, her red braid flopping on her shoulder. Mrs Rasmussen was standing guard by the telephone, an invention she admired for its instant transmission of bad news but distrusted because she could not see the other person. 'It's a man,' she hissed. 'From Canada. I couldn't catch the name...do you think it's the one with the blond hair that you met up by the river one day? So handsome...' And Mrs Rasmussen clasped her hands to her substantial bosom.

Deeply grateful that Mrs Rasmussen spoke very little English, Marya took the receiver and gasped, 'Hello.'

The line was hissing louder than Mrs Rasmussen, the hisses interjected with crackles like electricity. *'Hello,'* Marya repeated, and thought in utter despair, He's been cut off.

'Marya? Is that you? I want to speak to Marya Hansen, please...can you hear me?'

'It is Marya!' she shouted, and heard the words echo back to her down the receiver.

'My God,' said Craig. 'Is it really you?'

Because of the echo, she had to strain for every word. 'Yes, it's me,' she said inanely.

'I talked to this old——' crackle, crackle '—boy who at least spoke——' crackle, crackle '—are you?'

'It's a terrible connection,' she yelled. 'I can only hear a quarter of what you're saying.'

Through the echo and the crackling she heard only one word. '...quarter?' said Craig in great puzzlement.

'Never mind!' Marya took a deep breath, remembering how she had told Robb she had made a mistake in sending Craig away. That had been true, but it had been only a fraction of the truth: she had left out the most important part. With deep conviction she said, 'Craig, I love you.'

But an ululation like a coven of witches had now added itself to the crackling. '...another week, Marya, can you hear me? Operator, this damned phone is driving me crazy.'

That sentence, of course, Marya heard perfectly. She said, determined to get her message across, for she now knew it was the most momentous message in her life, 'Craig, I love you. Can you hear me? I made a mistake when I sent you away...I love you.'

'...love you...' said the echo. 'Operator!' said Craig. 'Marya, are you still——'

'I love you!' she shouted at the top of her lungs, and saw Mrs Rasmussen's gentian-blue eyes widen with delight.

For a moment there was a dead silence. '*What* did you say?' Craig demanded.

'I love you. I love you. I love you.'

Mrs Rasmussen drew a little closer, for drama like this did not come her way every day. Craig said, '...mean it?'

In a deafening crackle like a hundred lightning bolts the line went dead. Marya said desperately, 'Craig? Craig, are you there? Oh, God, he's gone...now what will I do?'

But she was speaking into an utter silence that made her sense with horrible immediacy the distance between them: an ocean and a vast land. And she was not at all sure that he had heard her.

'How romantic,' Mrs Rasmussen sighed. 'I remember when my first husband...' And she was away. Marya listened with half an ear, still clutching the receiver as if by sheer will-power she could conjure up Craig's voice at the other end. But the line stayed dead, and eventually she replaced the receiver on the hook.

'Wait a few moments, dear,' said Mrs Rasmussen. 'He might get through again. I'll make you a nice cup of tea and we'll have a ⬤⬤⬤ chat ... how pretty you look in that robe.'

Craig had kissed her in Magnus's kitchen when she was wearing this same robe. Abruptly Marya sat down. 'Thank you,' she said.

She drank tea she did not want, choked down a piece of coffee ring, dodged with varying degrees of success any number of awkward questions and prayed for the phone to ring. It remained obstinately and infuriatingly silent.

Half an hour later she went home.

Kathrin and Robb were thinking of being married in the medieval Olav church in Kirkjubøur. So a few days after the abortive telephone call Robb arranged for him and Kathrin, Marya, Grethe and Magnus to have dinner together in one of the hotels in Tórshavn and then drive the few miles south to Kirkjubøur to see the church.

Marya would have done almost anything to take her mind off Craig, from whom there had been no further phone calls and no letter; and she was quite happy to go to Kirkjubøur, for she had never been there with him and hence there would be no memories waiting to ambush her. But a few minutes before they were due to leave, when she slipped into Grethe's kitchen in her pretty sun-dress with a handwoven shawl over her shoulders, any chance she might have had of pleasure in the outing was shattered.

Robb was talking in the living-room; rooted to the spot, Marya listened. 'Kathrin just phoned the airport in Vágar,' he was saying. 'Craig wasn't on the plane.'

'He told you he'd be on it,' said Grethe. 'Where could he be?'

'Something must have happened to delay him. And there's not another plane until tomorrow.'

Kathrin's voice sounded frightened. 'Maybe he's been hurt—you said some of the union members might get tough, Robb.'

Robb sounded none too happy himself. 'I'll try and get through to his company from the hotel, and see if they know whether he left Vancouver as planned. In the meantime don't breathe a word to Marya, she'll only worry herself sick. As far as she's concerned this is a family outing and nothing more. Nothing to do with Craig.'

Marya very quietly let herself out of the door, and for a few moments stood on the step, trying to get herself under control. So the dinner had been arranged for six, not five, and the sixth was to have been Craig.

But Craig had not arrived, and no one knew why.

In her mind's eye she saw again the circle of men with their fists clenched, saw them surround Craig, saw him go down under a rain of blows...her breath caught in her throat and she squeezed her eyes tight shut to banish this nightmare vision. But closing her eyes only made the visions more vivid. He was in a hospital bed somewhere and nobody had thought to let his brother know. Or he was lying in a ditch by a lonely logging road, left for dead.

Her nails were biting into her palms; this way, she knew, lay madness. Clamping down on her imagination, she sent a desperate prayer heavenwards for Craig's safety. Then she gripped the door-knob, schooled her features to normality, and with all the pride and courage that Craig had admired in her walked back into the house. 'Are you ready?' she called.

Kathrin put her head around the living-room door. 'Ready and waiting,' she said in a sprightly voice, appearing to notice nothing out of the ordinary in her sister's face. 'I love your dress, Marya.'

Kathrin and Robb drove to the hotel in Robb's car; Marya drove Grethe and Magnus in Kathrin's. Driving gave Marya something to do. When they arrived at the hotel, she pretended not to notice that their table had been laid for six, ignored Robb's ten-minute absence from the table and the tiny shake of his head to Kathrin when he returned, and turned her back on the view through the window of the ferry *Norróna*, which had docked that afternoon from Bergen.

She chose duckling as her main course and made animated conversation with Magnus, minus his wool cap, and Grethe, who was delighted with this unexpected treat. The meal was, she supposed, delicious, and she even managed to eat at Kathrin's urging a very rich dessert; then they all left the hotel.

The tiny settlement of Kirkjubøur nestled on the shore, the islands of Hestur, the Horse, and Koltur, the Colt, bathed in the golden light of the westering sun across a placid stretch of water. The church, plain, whitewashed, was within a stone's throw of a rocky beach; behind it loomed the stark stone walls of the old cathedral, begun in the thirteenth century but never completed, its roof open to the sky, its arched windows blank of expression.

Dutifully Marya trailed after the others, scarcely listening to Kathrin's ebullient chatter and Robb's deep-voiced replies. Grethe was dreamily planning the wedding; Magnus was getting restless. Finally Kathrin said, 'Well, have we seen enough?'

Magnus made a beeline for the car. Marya said with an assumed calm of which she was rather proud, 'Would you all mind going back in one car? I think I'll stay here for a while, it's so peaceful.'

Kathrin gave her a sharp look and Robb said heartily, 'Rather late, isn't it, Marya?'

Maybe they suspected that she had overheard the conversation at Grethe's; maybe she had not been able to hide the tension that even now screamed along her nerves. Calling on all her dubious powers as an actress, Marya teased, 'Come on, you two, you get lots of time alone—it won't hurt you to drive Pa and Grethe home. And I won't stay that long.'

Not giving them the chance to argue, she set off across the grass past the nine-hundred-year-old outbuildings with their turf roofs to the uncompromising rectangle of the cathedral. To her infinite relief she heard their voices recede, then the beep of the horn as Robb drove away; casually she waved at them over her shoulder.

A red and white cow was grazing in the field behind the cathedral, and two black sheep scuttled away from her; the walls, four feet thick, were crusted with blue-green lichen. She went inside, where angelica flourished in the corners; the only other decoration the cathedral boasted were the weeds that grew in the gaps in the stone walls. The place was cold and silent with the weight of centuries, and brought her no comfort.

Pulling her shawl around her, Marya went outside. An eider duck was chivvying her young among the rocks, ripples spreading in water that was glazed with palest pink and delicate gold. She sat down, leaning against the whitewashed wall of the church, feeling the last warmth of the sun on her cheeks. When she closed her eyes, her lids glowed gold. The only sound was her own breathing.

Savage as a winter storm, all the anxiety she had been smothering for the last few hours rose up and overwhelmed her; and with it came the recognition that she was vulnerable again. This, she now knew, had been her true fear ever since she had met Craig, and it was from this that she had been running. Not from a rich man, not from Craig himself, but from the terrible cost of love. The other side of love, she thought bleakly. The side no one talked about. The black side.

With all her strength she wrestled with her fears, fighting to subdue them, striving to replace them with love. She loved Craig, loved him with all her heart. If anything could keep him safe, surely that could...if anything could bring him back to her, it had to be the power of love.

Time passed. When Marya finally opened her eyes, the sun was behind the cliffs of Koltur and the grass was cool and damp. She felt drained and empty and very tired. Yet she knew her inner struggle had been worthwhile: that somehow she had won a major victory. She still did not know if Craig was safe; she did know that loving him was the most important thing in her life, far outweighing the perils of vulnerability.

She could go home now, she thought. Perhaps there would be a message from Craig waiting for her.

Then a car door slammed behind the old wooden outbuildings, and she realised it had been the crunch of tyres on the dirt track that had brought her back to reality. With a twinge of resentment she knew she did not want to share the quiet of evening or her hard-earned peace with anyone else.

So when a man walked around the corner of one of the old buildings, her face was distinctly unfriendly. Craig stopped in his tracks and said with a quizzical lift of his brow, 'That's exactly how you looked in Toronto the first time I saw you.'

In rapid succession Marya's expression registered shock, disbelief, fear and happiness. She sat up, the stones of the church digging into her back, her heart beginning to race in her breast. 'Am I dreaming?' she whispered. 'Are you real?'

He came closer, then stooped, sitting back on his heels in the grass only a foot away from her. He was wearing bush trousers and a long-sleeved chamois shirt in a shade of deep green, and there were circles of exhaustion under his eyes. Struggling to catch her breath, Marya added inconsequentially, 'You've had a haircut.'

'Past due.' He gave her a crooked smile. 'Hello, red-haired woman.'

He *was* real, right here beside her where he belonged. Her prayers had been answered; he was safe. Flooded with mingled joy and gratitude, Marya gave him a tremulous smile back. Somehow, now that he was here, there was no hurry; there would be all the time in the world to tell him everything she needed to say. 'Welcome home, Craig.'

'Home is wherever you are,' he said, and, leaning his palms on the wall on either side of her head, he kissed her. Although her lips were chilled from the evening air, by the time he raised his head they were soft and moist and yielding. He traced the curve of her lower lip with one finger. 'I've been waiting for this for weeks,' he said. 'Years, it sometimes seems. Marry me, Marya?'

'Yes,' she said.

His eyes were filled with tenderness. 'A woman of few words.'

'The right word, I trust?'

'Absolutely...I think it calls for another kiss.'

This kiss was longer and deeper and called up, for Marya at least, some very explicit memories. 'To think that I asked if you were real!' she said, her cheeks pink. 'You haven't forgotten a thing.'

'I should hope not.' His gaze wandered over her face with a possessiveness she found highly satisfactory. 'This is, I suppose, where I should say that you're more beautiful than I remembered. You *are* beautiful. But you're also as pale as a ghost and much too thin.'

She ran her fingertip along his cheekbone to the fan of lines at the corner of his eye. 'And you look tired,' she said.

'I am. All the airlines between Vancouver and here seemed intent on keeping you and me apart. I was supposed to have joined you for dinner at the hotel, but a two-hour delay in Toronto and a bomb threat in Heathrow made me miss my connections.'

For a moment remembered terror shadowed her eyes. 'I overheard Robb and Kathrin, so I knew you were supposed to have joined us...I had you beaten up in the woods by a bunch of lumberjacks.'

Craig said calmly, 'There were a couple of guys who might have had ambitions in that direction. But I made sure I stayed out of their way. I had unfinished business, Marya, and the lumberjack isn't born who was going to keep me from that.'

Another smile tugged at her lips, for she was almost sure she was the unfinished business. 'So how *did* you get here?'

'I chartered a plane. And no rude remarks about rich men.'

'I wouldn't think of it.' With immense contentment she added, 'You missed a great dessert. Oh, Craig, it's wonderful to see you, and I'm so sorry I sent you away.'

'Not one of the best days of my life,' he concurred ruefully.

Her brow furrowed; it seemed very important that she make him understand. 'It was as though I had to be without you in order to really see you as you are. When you were here, you were too close, too immediate—and,' she added, looking at him through her lashes, 'much too distracting. It was only when you'd gone that I knew that Tony was totally unimportant and that I'd done you a terrible disservice to ever compare you with him. I *am* sorry.'

Her face was troubled. He said, 'You're forgiven. If indeed there's anything to forgive. I know I put a lot of pressure on you, Marya—it had all happened so fast, and I was so afraid of losing you. Too much pressure, I'm sure.' His smile was wry. 'At least, so I was informed by my younger brother.'

'Kathrin was a little impatient with me, too.'

'They think we're made for each other.'

'Do you agree?'

'I know we are.'

There was another kiss, this one ending with Marya lying on the grass and Craig more or less on top of her. She said dreamily, 'Later I'll ask you about your work, and why you look so tired—Robb explained to me what you do, and that's another apology I owe you, that I never asked. Did it end the way you wanted it to, Craig?'

'Finally, yes. But it was a battle, and could have gone either way.' He stroked her hair back from her forehead. 'Will you mind the demands of my job, Marya?'

'Only when you're in danger.'

'No danger could compare to my losing you. I've never been as frightened in my life as when I got on that plane in Vágar and knew it would be carrying me away from you.'

He had given her the perfect openeing. 'The main reason I sent you away was because *I* was afraid,' she confessed. 'Scared out of my wits of being hurt again, of being rejected and left alone. So I did the rejecting before you could.' She still looked troubled. 'I know now that you're not like Tony—I knew it when you left, only I wouldn't admit it. You'll never abandon me as he did.'

'Not likely,' said Craig.

'And overhearing Robb showed me how full of risk life is—so when you love someone you become vulnerable.' With deep conviction she finished, 'But it's still better to love. That's the lesson you've taught me.'

'Better by far,' Craig agreed. 'We're both vulnerable, Marya. It's the price of love.' He hesitated. 'I'm only sorry I live so far from your home. But you can come here any time you want to, and Kathrin and Robb won't be that far away.'

'I'd live with you in the Gobi Desert,' Marya declared, as romantically as Mrs Rasmussen could have wished.

'I hope that won't be necessary.' Craig took her more comfortably in his arms, stroking her shoulder under the flimsy shawl. 'We could have a double wedding with Robb and Kathrin.'

'In the church that's about ten inches from your head.'

'It had better be soon,' he growled. 'We can't make love in the hotel in Eidi, everyone knows you there. Your father's house is out, as is Grethe's. And as for here, apart from any scruples about the proximity of the church, a very large cow has just come around the corner and is looking at us with considerable interest.'

Marya gave a rich chuckle. 'There's always the island—you'd better hope for calm seas.'

Craig suddenly dropped his bantering manner. His voice rough with emotion, he said, 'I love you, Marya...more than I can say. I'll need a lifetime to show you.'

Touched to the heart, she whispered, 'I love you, too.'

He kissed her again, a fierce and passionate kiss, throwing his thigh over her and pulling her hard against the length of his body. When he finally released her, their hearts were hammering in unison and Marya's eyes were deep pools of emotion. 'Words aren't much good, are they?' she said shakily. 'But, Craig, I love you so much.'

He smiled into her eyes, then pulled her to her feet. 'I came back here partly because I couldn't stay away, partly because Robb told me you looked as though you were going into a decline, and partly because I was almost sure you'd said those same words on the telephone—that telephone call had to be the most frustrating conversation in my entire life. Did you say them, Marya?'

She grinned. 'This is what I said.' Throwing her head back, she shouted as loudly as she could, 'I love you! I love you! I love you!'

The cow lumbered away in alarm, the eider duck gave an indignant squawk and Craig laughed out loud. 'No wonder the operator cut us off.'

'The whole village, you understand, now knows I'm in love.'

'Then let's go and spread the word that we're getting married,' he suggested.

Arms around each other, they wandered up the slope towards the road. The cow cautiously poked her nose round the corner of the church and began munching on the clumps of grass that grew against the wall. The eider duck edged the chicks up on a rock to roost. And the last wash of pink on the sea turned to purest gold.